"I Didn't Make The Rules,"

she said defensively, "but I've had to live with them all my life. Society still judges a woman by a strict standard. And, whether I like it or not, I intend to measure up, if only for the sake of my job and my son."

"Caroline," Greg said, "I'm in no state to argue about this right now. Anything I say is going to come out sounding like I'm only interested in getting you into bed any way I can, and that's not true. Won't your...code of ethics stretch to going out to dinner with me?"

She almost gave in. Only the knowledge that what lay between them would never stop at dinner gave her the strength to refuse. "I can't. Please don't ask me again."

She hung up a moment later. And then she lay staring up at the ceiling. Never, in all her years of being a single parent, of putting herself through school, of facing classrooms full of hypercritical teenagers, had she felt so completely alone.

Dear Reader:

Series and Spin-offs! Connecting characters and intriguing interconnections to make your head whirl.

In Joan Hohl's successful trilogy for Silhouette Desire— *Texas Gold* (7/86), *California Copper* (10/86), *Nevada Silver* (1/87)—Joan created a cast of characters that just wouldn't quit. You figure out how *Lady Ice* (5/87) connects. And in August, "J.B." demanded his own story—*One Tough Hombre*. In *Falcon's Flight*, coming in November, you'll learn *all* about...?

Annette Broadrick's *Return to Yesterday* (6/87) introduced Adam St. Clair. This August *Adam's Story* tells about the woman who saves his life—and teaches him a thing or two about love!

The six Branigan brothers appeared in Leslie Davis Guccione's *Bittersweet Harvest* (10/86) and *Still Waters* (5/87). September brings *Something in Common*, where the eldest of the strapping Irishmen finds love in unexpected places.

Midnight Rambler by Linda Barlow is in October—a special Halloween surprise, and totally unconnected to anything.

Keep an eye out for other Silhouette Desire favorites— Diana Palmer, Dixie Browning, Ann Major and Elizabeth Lowell, to name a few. You never know when secondary characters will insist on their own story....

All the best,

Isabel Swift
Senior Editor & Editorial Coordinator
Silhouette Books

MARY ALICE KIRK
In Your Wildest Dreams

Silhouette Desire

Published by Silhouette Books New York

America's Publisher of Contemporary Romance

SILHOUETTE BOOKS
300 East 42nd St., New York, N.Y. 10017

ISBN: 0-373-05387-8

First Silhouette Books printing November 1987

America's Publisher of Contemporary Romance

Printed in the U.S.A.

MARY ALICE KIRK

is a full-time writer who holds degrees in American Studies and International Relations. Throughout her life she has been driven by creative energies, but she refused a scholarship in the performing arts to pursue an academic career. Although she enjoys many hobbies, the need to write stories about people is the most compelling force in her life and, along with her family, the thing from which she derives her deepest satisfaction. She also writes under the name of Jean Fauré.

To Peter, Finny, and David, beloved eggs,
who with paper airplanes, buckets of crayfish,
flies taped to windowpanes,
and enough messy diapers to single-handedly
keep Pampers in business,
make life so very interesting.

One

―――

"Caroline, are you still there?"

The red pen paused in midstroke above the page as Caroline Forrester looked up toward the black box hanging on the classroom wall. "Yes, Glenda?"

"Oh, thank God, you haven't gone yet." Glenda Malcomb's disembodied voice coming over the intercom was clearly relieved. "There's a Mr. Gregory Lawton here in the office who wants to talk to Sally Stimpson, but she's left for the day. Can you see him?"

Caroline checked her watch. "Do you know what it's about? I'm on my way out the door."

"He's got a permission slip for the sex education course in his hand," the school secretary replied ominously. "And he doesn't look happy."

Caroline blew her bangs off her forehead and frowned. What a way to end the week—listening to an incensed parent accuse her of promoting promiscuity among today's young people. But as one of the two health education teachers at Martha Custis Senior High, she'd been working for four years to get approval to teach the human growth and development course the way she and her team-teacher, Sally Stimpson, thought it ought to be taught. Tired or not, it was her job to soothe any ruffled feathers the unit on effective parenting might cause. Trouble was, it ruffled enough feathers to stuff a dozen mattresses. And if she weren't very diplomatic and very sure of herself, those feathers would end up being used on her when she was run out of town on a rail.

"Send him down," she told Glenda, then quickly changed her mind. "No, wait! Let me come up there. I'll talk to him in the lounge."

"Will do."

The intercom clicked off, and Caroline took a moment to secure the knot of honey-brown hair at her neck before she placed the stack of papers she'd been grading into her briefcase. Rising, she adjusted the belt of her madras shirtwaist dress and slung the strap of her pocketbook over her shoulder. Then she walked down the hall toward the main office, hoping that this meeting wouldn't take long. She'd been too busy to eat lunch, and the rumbling of her stomach was audible over the click of her low heels on the tile floor.

As she walked through the doorway to the office, she gave the secretary a questioning look. Without rising from her desk, Glenda nodded her head in the direction of the lounge. The long-suffering roll of her eyes told Caroline she'd better not keep Mr. Lawton waiting.

The lounge was directly behind the main office, a haven for harried and exhausted teachers, where students were forbidden to enter. When Caroline opened the door of the closed room, she grimaced at the lingering smell of smoke and the sight of empty lunch bags littering the tables. The room was deserted except for the tall sandy-blond man who was pacing back and forth in front of the bulletin board.

"Mr. Lawton?"

He turned at the sound of her voice, seeming to spear her with his gaze. Caroline shivered a little under the impact of his stare and registered two facts: he was very attractive, and he was very angry. She gave him her best professional smile, but she never got to extend her hand in greeting or even offer her name.

He strode toward her waving a crumpled piece of white paper and declaring, "I want an explanation, Mrs. Stimpson! I want to know when this school decided to teach hardcore pornography!" Coming to a stop close to her, his six-foot frame appeared to reach new heights. "I'm outraged!" he boomed. "How can you possibly justify what you're doing here? I won't stand for it! Monday morning I'm going to call the Board of Education. I'll speak to the superintendent! I'll see you all in court before—"

"Mr. Lawton, did you come to the presentation last week?"

"...allow my tax money— What?" He stopped short, his hand making a quick trip across his jaw and around behind his neck. "I, uh, no. I was out of town and I... what presentation?"

His impatience as he waited for her response was notable, and Caroline congratulated herself on the calm, even tenor of her reply. "Last Wednesday night Mrs. Stimpson and I met with the parents of the children in our human growth and development sections and gave a presentation of the materials we'll be using in the effective parenting unit. We also answered questions for any parents who had concerns similar to yours." She saw him take in the information that she wasn't Sally Stimpson, his child's teacher, but he didn't allow his error to deter the angry flash in his clear gray eyes.

"Humph," he grunted, brandishing the white paper once more. "I can't imagine you've gotten many of these so-called permission slips signed. I'm certainly not going to—"

"Actually only three out of a hundred and ninety-seven were returned saying the child couldn't participate."

That stopped him. She could almost see the wheels turning. Gregory Lawton was beach-boy attractive, with the sort of handsomeness that was perpetually youthful. His jaw was angular, his mouth firm, and he had laugh lines that crinkled at the corners of his eyes. Everything about him reeked of America and apple pie, right down to the uniform he was wearing, which told Caroline he was a pilot for Transcontinental Airways. He didn't look like a man who enjoyed being different. In fact it seemed to make him intensely uncomfortable.

"Only three were unsigned?" he asked with a slight hesitation.

It was the hesitation that gave Caroline the clue she needed. He wasn't used to being irate and irrational any more than he was used to being an oddball. He was merely upset and worried. And that was something she could handle.

Thinking that her friend Sally would owe her one for this afternoon's piece of work, she said, "Mr. Lawton, let's sit down and talk about this." She indicated the grouping of vinyl couches and chairs in the middle of the room. When he eyed her skeptically, she smiled. "My name's Caroline Forrester, by the way. I teach health education with Sally Stimpson."

As though he suddenly realized how rude he'd been, Greg let out a long breath and rubbed his hands across his face.

"Lord, you must think I'm crazy. I've been out of town and—well, that's no excuse for my behavior. Mrs. Forrester, I'm sorry."

Caroline shook the large hand he offered, accepting his apology. "Think nothing of it, Mr. Lawton. I'm sorry Mrs. Stimpson isn't here to speak with you herself. If you'd rather talk to her, I can give you her home number."

"No, I don't want to bother her at home." He laughed once, dryly. "I've already bothered you, but I didn't know what else—"

"Let's sit down," she interrupted, not wanting him to have to apologize again. When he turned to comply with her suggestion, she gave the peanut butter crackers in the vending machine a hungry look and told herself that she wouldn't starve if she had to wait another hour to eat.

"Now," she began, seating herself in a chair opposite him, "how is it that you didn't know about the effective parenting unit? I take it you weren't informed about the curriculum or the meeting?"

"No, not really. It's not my daughter's fault, though. I'm a commercial pilot, and I've been in and out of town more than usual lately. I flew into Dulles this afternoon, and when I got home, I found this parent consent form taped to the refrigerator. I was—well, you've got a good idea by now how I felt." He gave her a sheepish look, obviously embarrassed at his outburst.

Caroline smiled encouragingly. "I'm sorry you missed the meeting. I can't show you the movies, but I can go over the materials with you and answer any of your questions about the course."

"Oh, I can't ask you to do that. It's late and—"

"Nonsense," she scoffed gently. "You obviously have concerns, and you can't very well sign that permission slip feeling the way you do right now."

Greg looked down at the paper, which was becoming increasingly rumpled in his clenched fist. "Honestly, Mrs. Forrester, I don't think there's much you can say that's going to convince me to sign this."

"That may be true," Caroline allowed. "But let me explain the course to you first. If you can't sign it then with a clear conscience, at least you'll have given it serious consideration."

He cocked one brow. "But what will my daughter have to sit through if I don't agree to let her take this course?"

"The alternate unit covers human embryology, birth defects and early childhood development," Caroline replied evenly. "It's an excellent course."

He met her gaze for a moment, and Caroline could sense him assessing her motives.

"But you think this effective parenting thing is better," he concluded finally.

She shrugged one shoulder. "Better is a relative term. And what I think personally isn't the issue."

"But I'd like to know what you think," Greg insisted.

Caroline hesitated. Offering her own opinion on this topic was a tricky business. Her principal, Frank Lupton, had moved heaven and earth to get clearance to include the unit in the science curricula, but he'd left it up to her and Sally to see to it that no parent sued, claiming the school was imposing values on the children it taught. In the affluent suburbs of Washington, D.C., such an event was not out of the realm of possibility; the parents in the Martha Custis school district took an exceptionally active interest in their children's education. And Greg Lawton was exactly the sort of parent Frank Lupton feared most: a hothead.

Or was he? Somehow Caroline didn't think so. He was far more uncomfortable about his behavior and lack of control than she. Her intuition told her to play it very straight with him.

Bluntly she stated, "I think sixteen-year-olds are in desperate need of the information we'll be presenting in the effective parenting unit."

"I agree," he nodded, then qualified the statement by saying, "but I think they should learn these things at home."

"Ideally, yes," Caroline nodded slowly. "Unfortunately too many parents are afraid to talk to their children about sex. Others pass along the essentials but don't have the resources available to them that we do and can't possibly impart as much actual information. And, as amazing as it may seem, some parents are genuinely ignorant of even the most basic facts."

She leaned forward in her chair, her wide blue eyes full of concern and sincerity. "Our effective parenting unit is not a course full of theories and possibilities, Mr. Lawton. We want to teach the students the practical considerations of day-to-day life. They'll learn how to make and keep a budget based on incomes from the area in which they live and on their own future plans. We'll show them movies about venereal disease and the effects of drinking on the human fetus. They'll be going on a field trip to Johns Hopkins Hospital in Baltimore where an expert will walk them through the infertility clinic and talk to them about options available for people with those special problems. And they'll spend four days in the classroom with a certified nurse-midwife who's going to talk to them about prenatal development and giving birth. Every movie, every field trip, all the course materials have been carefully screened. Believe me, Mr. Lawton, we have your child's best interest at heart."

Greg's wide mouth thinned into a straight line, and Caroline could see he was making a considerable effort not to explode. He looked down at the permission slip, which he'd been folding and unfolding while she spoke. "And you really believe these kids need to hear these things? You don't think telling them all this is going to make sex seem very appealing and very available? It seems to me you're giving them a lot of power over something they won't know how to handle."

"On the contrary." She shook her head. "Other school systems that have developed and taught a curriculum like this one did studies that show that the exact opposite is the case. When teenagers are given *all* the information about the consequences of their bodies' sexual functioning, they tend to exercise more control over their behavior. The information gives them power, yes, but not in the way you're suggesting. Rather, it allows them to make intelligent choices. They aren't able to act impulsively and then excuse themselves later by saying that they didn't know any better."

Caroline sensed that the man opposite her was becoming less sure of himself by the second. She watched as he set the permission slip on the coffee table and raked a hand through his hair. Then leaning forward, he rested his elbows on his spread knees and clasped his hands together. Two seconds later he unclasped them and rubbed absently at the back of his neck with one hand while the fingers of the other drummed against his thigh. Caroline found all this nervous gesturing oddly endearing. Here was this big, gorgeous hunk of a man squirming in his seat as he wrestled with his conscience. Somehow, the outward signs of his inner battle appealed to Caroline far more than any deliberately flirtatious gesture he might have made. Statistics impressed him, that much was clear. What was becoming even clearer was that he didn't know what to do.

Caroline knew that feeling all too well. Rob was almost seventeen now; she'd raised him alone from the time he was six—or, more accurately from his birth, since one could hardly call Chuck's behavior parenting. She knew what it meant to face the hard decisions regarding a child's education and moral training. There were no easy answers.

"I don't know," Greg shook his head. "I've got to admit I've put off talking to my daughter about this stuff about as long as it can be put off. Maybe I am scared, as you've said. But I still would rather tough it out myself and have the satisfaction of knowing what she's heard and what her questions really are. And I'd like some control over the amount of information she gets. I guess I still think sixteen is very young to handle all the details your course seems to cover. And where does responsibility come into the picture? How can you possibly teach them that?"

Caroline grinned. "That's what the egg is all about."

He blinked. "The what?"

Chuckling at his look of disbelief, she explained, "The students have been split up into pairs of one boy and one girl. Each pair will be given a raw egg for which they'll be entirely responsible for nine weeks. They aren't allowed to put the egg in a box and forget about it, either. At least one of the pair has to be caring for it at all times. If the egg breaks, they both flunk the course."

Greg's eyes widened. "That's the most ridiculous thing I've ever heard."

Caroline spread her hands wide. "Can you think of a better way to teach a sixteen- or seventeen-year-old what it's like to take care of a baby? You asked about responsibility. Our purpose in this unit is to give children information they'll need in order to become responsible adults. We're trying to give them life skills so that when they're ready to begin their own families, they'll have some idea about what they're getting into."

"And part of teaching them life skills is to set up this mock marriage with an egg as the star attraction? What's to stop them from taking all the other information you'll be feeding them and doing a little experimenting of their own?"

His gazed skimmed over her, as though to say, *Come on, lady, we know exactly what we're talking about here. And it's called sex.*

The change in him threw Caroline. This wasn't the endearingly confused parent whose indecision had tugged at her heart a few moments ago. This was an utterly confident man who was making a calculated use of his clearly extensive experience with women to produce a desired effect. And for a moment or two it worked. Caroline's heart skipped a beat, and she was forced to either lower her gaze or blush.

Choosing the former course, she hurried on to explain, "The egg experiment was developed some years ago. It's been used in a variety of forms all over the country and has been considered very successful. I know it seems that we're encouraging a level of intimacy far beyond that which a parent would want his or her child to have in a relationship at this age. But, Mr. Lawton, you'd be amazed at what really goes on as the experiment progresses. In fact the pressures of, uh, egg parenthood tend to make the situation much less attractive than it first appears."

One corner of Greg's mouth quirked upward. "Just like the real thing, huh?"

"That's the general idea."

Greg shook his head and sighed. "I still don't know...."

"Let me show you the handouts we're going to use," Caroline offered, reaching for her briefcase. "They'll give you a better idea of how the material will be presented."

She was routing through bunches of dittos when she was mortified to hear her stomach let out an especially loud growl. Hoping Greg hadn't noticed, she started to say, "These materials were prepared by—"

"Look," he said, cutting her off. "I'm being a real pain in the neck here. You should be home eating your dinner. I can come back Monday."

"No, the course starts Monday morning and this is really no trouble."

His hand reached out to cover hers. The contact startled her, and her gaze flickered to his, her eyes widening a little, questioning.

"Mrs. Forrester," he said, "it's obvious you're a dedicated teacher and that you believe in what you're doing. But I can't sit here and listen to your stomach growl while you answer my questions."

"I'm okay, really," Caroline tried to assure him. She didn't want him to leave with his concerns unaddressed. He was right; she was a dedicated teacher. She also had very personal reasons for wanting this course to be successful.

Greg gave her a mildly frustrated look. "Well, if you're going to be stubborn, at least let me take you across the street and buy you a sandwich and a cup of coffee."

"Oh, I couldn't," she began, pulling her hand out from beneath his.

"Yes, you could," he insisted. "Call it an apology for the idiotic way I came on at the beginning of this discussion. I'm not proud of myself, you know, losing it like that. And it's only going to make me feel worse to sit here watching you starve."

Put that way, she couldn't very well refuse. Caroline capitulated gracefully, stuffing the papers back into her briefcase and saying, "A cup of coffee sounds wonderful but if

I eat a sandwich, my son will shoot me for spoiling my dinner.''

He rose from the couch smiling. ''You've got one of those, too? To listen to my daughter, you'd think I was about three years old instead of forty-two. She's been that way since my wife died.''

The puzzle pieces clicked into place in Caroline's brain, and the picture made sense. He was a single parent. More than that, he was a man raising an adolescent daughter. He wasn't outraged at the idea of his child learning the facts of life. He was scared to death of what might happen to her if she didn't learn them properly. And if he weren't careful, he'd have every right to be scared.

Suddenly Caroline's desire to help Greg Lawton understand the importance of allowing his daughter to take the course increased a hundredfold. She didn't even try to deny to herself that she had a personal interest in helping the girl through her father. A teacher couldn't always be objective. Sometimes the very best teaching came from commitment born of personal and painful experience. Caroline hoped she'd be able to save the young Ms. Lawton a lesson or two from the school of hard knocks.

The after-school crowd had gone home and the dinner crowd hadn't yet hit when Caroline and Greg arrived at the deli. Caroline slid into a booth and waited while Greg bought two cups of coffee.

As he sat down opposite her, he smiled, saying, ''By the way, *Caroline*, given the topic we're discussing, I'd be a lot more comfortable if you called me Greg.''

Given the topic they were discussing, Caroline would have been a lot more comfortable not calling him anything at all. She would have preferred to keep things as distant and as clinical as possible. She was accustomed to talking about sex. She did it for a living. And she'd been going on now for half an hour, speaking to Greg Lawton confidently and without embarrassment. Up to this point her attention had been focused on defusing his anger and on getting him to hear her out; her concern had been for her job and his daughter and the course of study she'd worked so hard developing. But for some inexplicable reason, when he called her Caroline and smiled, it occurred to her that she couldn't remember the last time she'd talked about sex while sitting alone with a man. An attractive man.

"Are those for me to look at?"

Caroline dropped her gaze from Greg's face to the dittos she'd taken out to give to him. It was as though she'd never seen them before. Suddenly clinical became intimate. Professional became personal. And her confidence suffered under an onslaught of absurdly adolescent embarrassment.

"Uh, yes, they are," she replied, stammering in a way she hadn't in years.

Get it together, Caroline, she told herself sternly. *Be cool. Be understanding. Tell yourself he's only a worried father. And if it makes him more comfortable to have you call him Greg, do it. You'll survive.*

Thus fortified, for the following forty-five minutes Caroline gave Greg an overview of the entire effective parenting unit. She couldn't show him the movies and slides, but she did give him abstracts that described them. Greg asked good questions and did a remarkable job of withholding judgment on what he was seeing, some of which was very explicit.

He did, however, clear his throat an awful lot. Which didn't help Caroline at all. Every time he laughed or in any way acknowledged the personal nature of the topic they were discussing, she was reminded that he was a man and that she was a woman and that it was incredibly odd for them to be talking about the intimate details of sex when they'd known each other for less than two hours. Even longtime lovers seldom got around to discussing the topic so thoroughly.

What finally restored Caroline's sense of balance was Greg's unspoken but clear expectation that she would behave in a relaxed and confident manner. He didn't need her embarrassment. He certainly didn't need to be bothered with the abrupt and unwanted awakening of her dormant sexual awareness. In fact the more they talked, the more Caroline believed that what he needed most was some good, old-fashioned reassurance. Reassurance that his daughter would be all right, that even without her mother, she would grow into responsible adulthood. And Caroline couldn't help the feeling of sympathy that rose inside her. He was trying *so hard*! She thought about how many times she'd needed someone to pat her on the back and tell her Rob was going to be okay. She had to restrain the impulse to actually reach out and give Greg that pat, letting him know that his efforts were noticed.

When she'd finished going over the course syllabus, Greg looked more confused than ever. His words confirmed all her suspicions.

"Caroline, I swear I don't know what to do." He rubbed his hand across his face in what had already become a familiar gesture and looked again at the tabletop scattered with papers. "I've tried to be a good parent, but it seems all my daughter and I do these days is fight. I've been away so much it feels like I hardly know her anymore. Our housekeeper, Mrs. Reid, is wonderful—she's almost a member of the family after being with us for seven years—but I can't pass this job along to her. Discipline, money, religion. Sex. Those are things I need to teach my child myself, but it seems like I'm never there when she needs me the most. She wants more freedom, and I guess I'm just plain scared of giving it to her. The truth is she's a good kid and hasn't done a thing to make me distrust her. But I go, well, sort of crazy when I think about her being hurt by some punk with a case of overactive hormones. The one she's got hanging around her lately—some Rob character—every time I see him he's gaping at her like he wants to strip her naked! At least that's how it looks to me."

Caroline stiffened, all her sympathetic feelings evaporating in the face of purely maternal protectiveness. Her tone was carefully controlled as she asked, "What's your daughter's name?"

"Kimberly." Greg met her gaze briefly—then did a double take when he caught the narrow stare she was giving him. "Oh, Lord," he muttered. "What have I said wrong now?"

"That Rob character you mentioned happens to be my son," Caroline answered coolly. But at his look of distress, she couldn't maintain any real anger.

"I should never have left San Francisco this morning," Greg said, sighing. "You wouldn't happen to be teaching a course in how to avoid social blunders, would you? I think I need a refresher."

"Unfortunately that's one of those things they never teach you in school," Caroline replied, offering him a smile. "But don't worry, I've been a single parent myself for the past twelve years. I know how paranoid it makes you. And you're raising a girl. As much as we like to tell ourselves that the double standard is a thing of the past, the reality is, mistakes are more costly for girls than they are for boys. I don't envy you a bit. On the other hand—" she smiled warmly "—I've seen Kimberly, though I didn't know her last name. If Rob's hormones have become overactive, I think you should blame yourself for producing such a lovely daughter." The little pixie with the heart-shaped face and the cap of blond curls had kept Rob entranced for several months now, Caroline knew, and she could understand why.

Greg took the compliment as it was intended, and Caroline saw him register the fact that she wasn't going to rush to her son's defense. She also saw him take in the information that she was single as his gaze slid briefly to her left hand. She'd seen other men perform that same reconnaissance; she didn't like it, but she resisted the urge to slide her hand under the table.

Wanting to keep the conversation focused on their children, she asked, "How long have you been raising Kimberly alone?"

"Almost five years," he answered. "Joanne, my wife, died of leukemia when Kim was twelve. She'd had the disease from the time Kim was six. In some ways Kim has had to grow up very quickly, but in others she's quite childish. I'm afraid I've encouraged that immaturity trying to compensate, I guess, for what I think her mother's illness stole from her childhood."

"You can't stop the growing-up process once it's started," Caroline commiserated. "Rob often astounds me with his maturity, but I feel guilty, too, sometimes that my divorcing his father has somehow forced him to grow up too fast."

Then as another thought struck her, she laughed softly. "I suppose I should warn you that if you decide to sign that permission slip, Kim and Rob are going to become proud egg parents together. At least that's Rob's intention. They're both in Sally Stimpson's fourth period class."

Greg's eyes widened. "Would that make us egg grandparents?"

"I guess so."

His warm gaze moved over her face. "You don't even look old enough to be the mother of a sixteen-year-old."

Caroline's smile turned to a flush of feminine awareness, and she looked down at her empty coffee cup. "Thank you, but I assure you I am. Look—" she glanced at her watch "—I really do have to be going now. Rob fixes dinner on Friday nights, and he'll be wondering where I am."

"Of course," Greg agreed, and began helping her gather the scattered papers. Holding up one especially detailed drawing for closer inspection, he shook his head. "What I don't understand is how the devil you can talk about this stuff all day long. Doesn't it get to you? I mean, even the *thought* of discussing human reproduction with Kim leaves me tongue-tied. And you talk about it like it's a recipe for chocolate chip cookies!"

Caroline took the paper from him and gave it an indifferent glance. Inwardly she was pleased her attack of the jitters had gone unnoticed. "You can't afford to be embarrassed when you're talking to sixteen-year-olds," she said with a casual shrug. "They'll get you every time."

"I know what you mean. Kim doesn't miss a trick." He cocked his head thoughtfully. "I can't believe, though, that she won't be embarrassed by all this. She's not shy, but, well..."

"But even the *thought* of discussing human reproduction with her leaves you tongue-tied," Caroline finished for him, laughing. "The surprising thing is that kids who are normally shy respond differently when the information is presented by someone other than a parent. The students will ask me all sorts of things they'd choke on before asking their mother or father."

Greg sighed. "I can't deny that it would be a relief to turn the whole messy topic over to Mrs. Stimpson and let her handle it. I only want to be sure in my own mind I'm not abdicating a responsibility I'll wish later I'd hung on to.

Meanwhile, however, I really appreciate your giving me this much of your time.''

"I hope I've been some help," Caroline said honestly, closing the briefcase and reaching for her purse.

"You've been a tremendous help. I've needed to have somebody listen to me talk about Kim, and I'm very grateful that somebody turned out to be you." His smile was touched with something other than simple gratitude, however, as he added, "You're a good listener, Caroline Forrester."

Determined not to acknowledge his look of male interest, Caroline replied flippantly, "Even if I have got a kid with overactive hormones who's got designs on your daughter?''

"I have a feeling," Greg began with a dry grimace, "that I've been looking at all males under the age of twenty-one with a jaundiced eye. Maybe Rob won't look so bad now that I've gotten some of the worry off my chest."

"And what about the course?" Caroline couldn't help asking. "What are you going to do?"

He waited for her to stand, then guided her through the crowd of people who had arrived in the past twenty minutes. As they walked out the door, he replied, "I don't know what I'm going to do. I want to talk to Kim this weekend and see what she has to say about it. But, you know—" his steps slowed a little as his eyes skimmed quickly but thoroughly over her slender form "—this whole egg thing is beginning to sound very appealing. I think I like the idea of being egg grandparents with you, Caroline."

Caroline kept her eyes straight ahead as she crossed the street. Greg Lawton was not interested in being egg grandparents with her. But the thing which *did* interest him was becoming all too apparent.

* * *

Greg walked to his car whistling. He felt better than he had in weeks. Some of that was because the flight he'd made that afternoon had marked the end of a grueling three months. His schedule over the next few weeks would be much easier. But he attributed the greater part of his newly achieved peace of mind to Caroline Forrester. He still had reservations about the whole sex education business, but something told him that his worries were unnecessary. Caroline Forrester would never involve herself in anything that wasn't completely respectable. Furthermore, he couldn't imagine anything in which she was involved being done incorrectly. He would rather Kim had been in Caroline's class than in Mrs. Stimpson's, whom he'd never met; but if Caroline endorsed Kim's teacher, that was good enough for him.

He'd talk to Kim about the course that evening, maybe take her out to dinner. They hadn't done anything like that together in a long while. And maybe his signing this permission slip could be the white flag of truce between them. They'd had a lot of fights lately, and he was more than willing to take the first step toward ending the battle for power. In fact there were quite a few steps he could take, like compromising on her demands to be allowed to date. If she didn't take his peace offerings in the manner in which they were intended or if she abused the privileges, well, he'd be around more and therefore able to keep an eye on things. Yes, he had the time now to sort out his relationship with his daughter.

In fact he even had the time to relax and enjoy himself a little. And as his thoughts drifted back to the afternoon, it occurred to him that he couldn't think of anyone with whom he'd rather spend some of that time than Caroline Forrester.

What would she think if he called her and asked her out to dinner? Had she been as completely aware of him as he'd been of her? His instincts told him yes, but he wasn't sure. Had she realized how hard it had been for him to listen to her talk about sex? Thank God she hadn't been able to read his mind, because he'd spent a good part of her proper little lecture translating all those drawings of body parts into living, breathing flesh curved into a shape that looked exactly like hers.

His attraction to her was more than physical, though. It had been a long time since he'd met a woman he'd liked so much on first sight. She was smart and funny and warm; and somehow, he knew she had understood exactly how he'd felt even when he hadn't been all that certain himself.

Yes, Caroline Forrester was a woman he'd like to get to know. If his hunch was correct, she's say yes to going out with him. If it was wrong, well, surely in the course of their nine weeks of shared egg grandparenthood, their paths would cross again.

Two

On Monday Caroline was pleased to learn that Friday afternoon's efforts had not been wasted. Sally informed her that they still had three students who would have to take the alternate unit but that a beaming Kimberly Lawton had produced her signed—if slightly mutilated—permission slip before school that morning. At the end of fourth period she and Rob had gone off cradling their egg in a shoe box and making excited plans for its care.

The enthusiastic response Caroline got from her classes that day added to her sense of accomplishment. There was plenty of moaning and groaning, and some students refused to take anything seriously. But it was all for show, Caroline knew. Though they'd never want her to find out, they were dying to get into the material.

By seventh period she was dead tired and didn't think she'd ever be able to look at another egg; but she was happy. It filled her with satisfaction to be doing the sort of teaching she'd dreamed about when she'd been a scared twenty-three-year-old divorcée with a little boy in first grade and no skills besides typing learned in high school. Things hadn't looked good. It was amazing how far a person could get on determination alone.

"Ms. Forrester, how are you going to know we didn't break the egg and replace it?"

Caroline looked over the box of eggs on her desk toward Skip Johnson. "Believe me, Skip, we've got that angle covered. These little darlings have numbered, tamperproof decals wrapped around their middles. I've already got a number assigned to you and Jenny."

Skip groaned. Jenny shot him a look across the room, rolling her eyes.

Caroline went on. "Before I hand out the eggs, I'm going to go over the list of rules you've been given. The egg cannot be left alone or kept in a sealed container. On the numbered band around the egg you'll find a temperature indicator. Your job is to prevent the egg from either cooking or freezing by keeping the indicator in the middle, blue range. Use your common sense about this. If you're hot, so is the egg. It's up to you and your partner how you work out caring for the egg, but keep in mind you're expected to share the responsibility. The only homework you'll have for the next nine weeks will be the daily log you'll be keeping about your egg. The statistical part of the log you'll do with your partner. The paragraph or two that you write at the end of each week telling me your concerns and feelings about the project will be confidential between you and me. So if you're having problems with your partner, you can write this without fear that he or she will find out. Corey, sit down in your seat. Mark, do you have a question?"

"Can we change partners after the project starts?"

"There will be no divorces," Caroline decreed. "You've had two months to make your choice, and you're in it for the long haul. As you know, your parents have been asked to fill out two progress reports during the course of this experiment. These will be sent home during the third week of April and the third week of May. The purpose of these reports is to give me an idea of how much time you actually spend caring for your egg and how seriously you go about your parenting duties." Caroline paused and scanned the youthful faces before her. "Are there any other questions?"

Theresa Calderone raised her hand. "Can we leave the egg with somebody besides us?"

"Yes," Caroline said, nodding. "But remember sitters have to be paid."

"With *money*?" Carl Jenkins was aghast.

"That's the usual practice," she replied, trying to hide a smile. "But it's fine to barter time or services if you can't afford the going rates. Of course, if you're out with a friend for the evening and the friend offers to watch the egg while you go into a store or to a rest room, well, that's a little different. The point is not to take advantage of a friend's generosity too often."

The enthusiasm was already waning, Caroline noted, as the reality set in. "Keep in mind," she added, "no matter who you leave the egg with, it's you who is responsible for it. If you leave it with your six-year-old sister and she breaks it, you and your partner are the ones who will flunk. Yes, Lisa?"

Lisa Turner gave her a wide-eyed, innocent look, which was lost amidst layers of mascara. "Ms. Forrester, aren't these eggs going to get rotten?"

The question generated an undercurrent of giggles and wisecracks throughout the room, and Caroline waited for the ruckus to die down before she answered.

"Probably. But they won't smell unless you break them."

Then, picking up her grade book, she moved on. "Okay, if that's all the questions, come up when I call your name, and I'll give you your egg."

The distribution went smoothly and by two-thirty Caroline had gotten everyone out of the room with their eggs in one piece. At three o'clock she met Rob in the parking lot to go home.

"Hi!" he called, pushing his lanky form away from the hood of their car as she walked toward him. He was already taller than she by half a head with the promise of more inches to come.

"Hi, yourself," Caroline replied, giving him a weary smile and dumping the keys into his outstretched hand. Rob had gotten his license almost nine months ago but driving was still a novelty in which Caroline was perfectly willing to indulge him.

Rob started talking the minute they were in the car. "Did Mrs. Stimpson tell you Kim's dad signed the permission slip? How come you didn't tell me you'd met him on Friday?"

"I didn't think it was any of your business," Caroline replied, thinking for at least the hundredth time that week that she wished he'd get his hair cut. Light brown locks were hanging over the collar of his blue jeans jacket, and she resisted the urge to smooth them back as if he were seven and not nearly seventeen.

"What do you mean it isn't any of my business?" Rob gave her an astonished look with eyes as blue as her own.

"Watch the road," she directed absently. "I mean just what I said. A parent came to me to discuss his daughter's education. It wouldn't be any more professional for me to tell you about that discussion than it would be for me to tell you what grade someone got on a test.''

"Yeah," Rob said, grimacing, "but you know I'm interested in Kim.''

An image of Greg Lawton's face as he told her about the punk with the overactive hormones flashed in Caroline's mind, and she chuckled. "Yes, I know you're interested in Kim.''

"What's so funny?''

"Never mind.''

Slightly disgruntled, Rob went on, "Well, whatever you said to Mr. Lawton, I wish you'd say some more of it. He really does a number on Kim, and I think she's had about all she can take.''

Feeling very defensive on Greg's behalf, Caroline said, "Go easy on him, Rob. I'm sure he's doing the best he can.''

"Maybe," Rob grumbled. "But his best is positively ancient history. He's got Kim feeling like she's some kind of freak. I've been wanting to ask her out for months but she isn't allowed to date. It's *killing* us!''

Caroline frowned. "What do you mean she isn't allowed to date?''

"Just what I said. No movies. No parties. No guys over to her house. She's got her own car for going back and forth to school, but she can't take it any place else. And she can't ride in guy's cars at all! I'm telling you, he treats her like she's about two years old.''

"More like twelve," Caroline mumbled, remembering how old Greg had said Kim was when her mother had died. It seemed as though things were a lot more serious than Caroline had imagined. If what Rob had said were true—and she didn't doubt that it was—it was amazing that Greg had given his permission for Kimberly to take the effective parenting unit. It must have required a monumental leap of faith on his part to reach such a decision. And from the sound of it, that faith had been in her. Caroline didn't know whether to be flattered or scared.

"Well, anyway," Rob continued as he turned the car into the entrance of their townhouse development, "I'd sure like to be able to ask her out."

"Have you suggested double-dating?"

"Yeah. The answer's no."

"How about inviting him to go somewhere with you and Kim?"

Rob shot her a look of disbelief. "Are you kidding?"

Caroline shrugged. "Actually I thought it was a pretty good idea. Mr. Lawton isn't an unreasonable man, Rob. He's only worried about his daughter. Getting to know you would help a lot."

"You really think so?"

"Yes, I do."

Rob was silent for a moment, then began hesitantly, "I'd be willing to do that. But it sure makes me nervous, thinking about taking a girl out with her father riding in the back seat. I mean, well, would you—if I asked him to go some place with us, that is—would you come with us?"

Caroline blinked once, then began a frantic search for a means of escape from the trap into which she'd fallen. "Oh, Rob, I couldn't—"

"Please, Mom." He pulled the car to a stop in front of their modest, red-brick townhouse and turned to her. "He likes you. Kim says so. It wouldn't be like a date but more like a goodwill gesture, you know? And it'd only be this once. Please."

Greg Lawton liked her? His daughter had said so? What had he said to make Kim think that? And what was *she* doing getting the information from the high school grape-vine?

Caroline looked at her son's big blue eyes and tried to remember when she'd ever been able to refuse him. There had never been a time, not when his request was absolutely reasonable and within her power to grant.

"All right," she said with great reluctance.

"All *right*!" he shouted triumphantly.

"But just this once."

"You got it, Mom," he agreed as he bounded from the car and up the front walk, calling back to her, "This is great!"

Just great, Caroline thought dismally as she got out of the car. At the age of thirty-five she'd sunk to letting her son fix her up with his girlfriend's father. And the worst part was that she was vastly disappointed that Greg Lawton wasn't somebody she could see socially on a continuing basis. It seemed to her that she was long overdue for a real date. But then, she was long overdue for a lot of things that had to do with her own needs and desires. Instinct told her, though, that Greg Lawton was exactly the sort of man she should avoid at all costs. She simply couldn't afford the risk he posed. Not yet, anyway.

"Hang on, Mom! You're going to break your neck!"

Caroline turned her head very slowly and shot her son a scathing look. Then, inch by inch, clutching the railing to her left, she made her way along the outside of the roller rink until she could sink down onto the bench nearest the rink entrance. Her mistake had been in putting the skates on before she'd reached the bench. No, she corrected herself, her mistake had been in agreeing to participate in this fiasco in the first place.

Roller-skating! Of all the things Rob could have chosen to do on his first date with Kimberly Lawton! What had happened to drive-in movies? Where were the pizza parlors and jukeboxes? Judging from the crowd and the noise level at the roller rink, the hangouts of yesteryear must be deserted. The jukeboxes had definitely been replaced with the sounds of the twenty-first century, and Caroline didn't see a jukebox anywhere.

She looked down at her skate-clad feet, which felt like they didn't quite belong to the rest of her, and wondered where all the years had gone and where she'd been while they were passing. She couldn't have been feeling more her age when Greg came skating toward her. He'd gotten his skates on first and had gone to check out the surface of the rink. The surface and what was on it looked pretty good to her, Caroline thought with a little shiver of excitement as she watched Greg glide across the brightly lit rink. He moved with remarkable grace for a man of his height and muscular build, which made her feel all the more like a klutz. And to add insult to injury, he had a huge grin on his face.

"I have to give your son credit," Greg said, plopping down on the bench beside her. "He knows how to have a good time."

"Hmmm," Caroline mumbled noncommittally.

Before Greg could comment on her lack of enthusiasm for the evening's activity, his daughter came walking over, skates in one hand and shoe box in the other. Inside the box, snuggled deep in a nest of cotton padding, rested egg number 1865.

"I hope you don't mind going skating, Ms. Forrester," Kim said as she sat down on Caroline's other side. She placed the shoe box on the floor beneath the bench and began putting on her skates. "Rob knows how much I love to skate. It was sweet of him to bring me, but maybe we should have checked with you first."

Unable to burst Kim's bubble of delight at being out with a boy, for the very first time, Caroline smiled. "Not at all, Kim. This was a fine idea."

"See, I told you it was okay." Rob came bouncing up to the group. With amazing speed he shucked his high tops and laced his skates, asking, "You gonna try it, Mom?"

At a loss for words Caroline stammered, "Uh, well, sure! But it's, um, awfully crowded out there, isn't it?"

Rob glanced briefly at the packed rink. "Naw, there's plenty of room. Give it another hour, and you'll really see some action. Let me know if you need help, okay?" Then, grabbing Kim's hand, he stood and looked down at her expectantly.

She, in turn, nodded and tossed her father a charming smile before gliding gracefully off with her new beau.

"You're a great liar, Caroline. Anybody ever tell you that?"

Caroline turned to meet Greg's twinkling gaze. "What? You don't believe I'm simply thrilled to be here?"

He arched one brow dubiously. "Sorry, but you look a little like the people I flew in this morning from Denver. We ran through a big storm, and they were kind of green by the time we landed."

"Go on," she scoffed. "I'm not that bad."

"Close."

"Well . . ."

"You ever skated before?"

"Nope."

"You gonna try?"

"Nope."

"Aw, come on, Caroline. I'll hold your hand."

"Forget it."

"Scared you'll fall?"

"You bet."

"I'll catch you."

"Ha!"

"Hey! Watch it, will you? You're bruising the ego here."

"Better your ego than my..."

The heat crept up her face slowly as the silence stretched.

Greg chuckled with devilish, knowing amusement. "Is this the same lady who spent two hours with me last Friday making Dr. Ruth sound like Miss Susan on Romper Room?"

"No, that lady is out to lunch. What you see is only a reasonable facsimile."

Greg's voice was silky and low as he said, "Looks like a good imitation to me. All the same beautiful qualities. And a few nice extras." His finger touched her cheek lightly. "This lady blushes. I like that."

Caroline's eyes widened as she felt herself shiver at his unexpected touch. With a jolt she realized what it was about Greg Lawton that made her wary and nervous. He was making a pass at her, not a crude one but a very nice one in fact. It wasn't the first time a man had done that to her. And he wasn't the first attractive man she'd been out with over the past twelve years. But he was the first one whose masculinity had struck such a resonant chord inside her. He'd barely touched her, but, as ridiculous as it seemed, she was feeling as nervous as if it were *she* who was the teenager out on her first date.

Knowing her feelings were totally out of proportion to the situation, Caroline looked around quickly for a distraction. Her eyes fell on the cardboard shoe box.

"Oh, heavens!" she exclaimed in genuine distress, bending to retrieve the box. "Somebody's going to kick this if it stays on the floor."

"Don't you touch that box," Greg ordered. "I've had all I can take this week of that damned egg. I almost wish it would break and get it over with. This is the first time it's been out of Kim's hand since Monday afternoon. I think she sleeps with it on her pillow."

Caroline frowned. "I wondered why Rob hadn't brought it home. He should be sharing the responsibility."

"I think he takes care of it all day in school," Greg explained. "I suppose that's really the harder job. There must be more opportunities for disaster in a cafeteria lunch line or a crowded hall than there are in Kim's bedroom."

Still frowning, her eyes on the box under the bench, Caroline said, "They shouldn't have left it here. I don't mind watching it, but—"

"They shouldn't have assumed we'd take care of it," Greg interrupted. "It was their job to make arrangements. Isn't that how the rules go?"

She nodded. "You're right. But I hate to spoil their evening. Kim looks so happy."

They both glanced across the rink at their children, who were still holding hands as they skated. Kim was laughing, and Rob was talking a mile a minute. Both were obviously enjoying themselves immensely.

"Rob's a nice boy," said Greg. "He's smart and well-mannered, and he isn't afraid to speak to an adult like one human being to another. He even drives like he's got good sense."

Caroline couldn't help but smile. "You have no idea how nervous he was about your being in the back seat. He's been worried for days about what he'd do if the parking lot was full and he had to parallel park on the street."

Greg laughed. "Thank God there was space in the lot. I wouldn't want to be the cause of him losing his cool. Not after the smooth way he handled inviting me to go out with him and Kim this evening.''

Pausing for a moment, Greg added more seriously, ''I'm sorry I've been so hard on Kim. She's been a different person this week, since I signed her permission slip and told her that she could go out with Rob. I've been making a big mistake in not trusting her, in not admitting she's growing up. I hope it's not too late to change.''

''I'd say the timing's about right,'' Caroline assured him.

Their eyes locked for a moment, and Greg's held a message of thanks. Then his looked changed. ''Speaking of timing, whadda ya say, Caroline? Are you gonna skate with me or not?''

She drew herself up straight. ''I told you, Greg, I'm not going to make a fool of myself.''

''I won't let you make a fool of yourself, I promise,'' he said earnestly. ''Besides, you aren't going to sit on this bench and baby-sit that damned egg! It's not your job and if they don't learn that now, the next eight weeks are going to be miserable.''

He was right about that much, Caroline knew.

Before she could say anything else, Greg called out to Rob and Kim who were skating nearby. The kids pulled to a stop.

''Is everything okay, Daddy?'' Kim asked hesitantly.

''Oh, everything's fine,'' Greg answered, getting to his feet and hauling a gasping Caroline up with him. ''I only wanted you to know that we're going to skate now. Thought you might want to do something about that little bundle of joy there on the floor. See you later.''

Then he clamped a strong arm around Caroline's waist and zoomed out onto the rink. Caroline, who was too scared to scream, had little choice but to latch on to him wherever she could. They'd gone about fifty feet when she found her voice.

"*Greg!* Are you crazy? Oh, Lord, don't let go! You've got to take me back right now, before I fall and *kill* myself!''

He laughed in good-natured amusement at Caroline's squeals and gasps, obviously enjoying himself to no end. In fact, it was disgusting how little effort it cost him to keep her upright as he propelled them around the rink. Miraculously, they didn't run into any of the other skaters, and he even managed to keep some sort of time with the music. While Caroline was busy clutching at him and making frantic pleas to be taken back to the bench, Greg was flying along the polished wooden floor telling her she was perfectly safe in his arms, that he had no intention of letting her go, and that she should relax and have a good time.

The crazy part was, that as they made their third pass around the rink, Caroline began to realize she *was* having a good time. She'd have fallen instantly if he hadn't been supporting her, and her feet were no more coordinated on the third go-round than they'd been on the first. But the fear of falling was rapidly being overshadowed by a tingling warmth spreading through her that could only be labeled *arousal*. The arousal came from her close proximity to Greg's beach-boy-sexy body.

His right hip was glued a little above her left one. His right arm was around her waist, his fingers spread across her ribs under her breast. She had a death grip on his free hand with one of hers while the fingers of her other hand dug into his left bicep. The last man who'd been this close to her was Ed Franklin, a friend of Sally Stimpson's husband, whom she'd dated six months ago. They'd gone dancing one night, and he'd taken the opportunity to try to seduce her. All he'd gotten for his efforts had been a bruised instep and a very clear refusal.

Greg Lawton was getting a lot more than a bruised instep. Caroline was sure her fingernails were drawing blood beneath his shirt, and she'd kicked him with her skates countless times. He was still laughing, though, and telling her she was doing fine. And she hadn't a thought of refusing him anything at the moment.

Then, on the fifth round, Greg spoke over the noise of music and laughter and wheels on wood. "Okay, now I want you to try standing up by yourself."

"No!" Caroline squealed, clinging on to him with renewed fervor. "Don't you dare let me go, Greg Lawton!"

"I'm not going to let you go," he told her calmly. "I'm going to hold your hands. See? That's it. Now, I'm only going to move away a few inches."

"Greg, I don't like this!"

"You're doing fine. I'm going to face you—like this—and I want you to try to skate toward me. Watch me, not your feet."

"I'm going to fall," her voice quavered.

"No, you're not."

"Yes, I *am*."

"I'll catch you before you do, I promise."

In creeping inches, biting her lower lip, Caroline began to try to skate. Skating backward in front of her, Greg held her hands and pulled her along. It was a tedious process, but Caroline was becoming determined to succeed. Greg made it look so easy, and she had a good sense of balance. There wasn't any reason she couldn't learn to do this. The thought that she *should* have learned years before weighed on her mind. There had been a lot of things she should have learned. Some of them were opportunities that were gone forever. But then, there were other things. Things like roller-skating.

On the sixth round Greg let go of one of her hands, and she didn't scream in protest. She didn't fall, either. On the seventh round, still holding her hand, he whirled around to skate beside her. On the ninth round she took the initiative to let go. Not for long—only a few seconds the first time. After a few minutes passed, she was finally able to go the length of the huge rink by herself. When she got to the turn, she reached for Greg's hand, and it was there. She was inordinately pleased with herself, but she didn't dare say so. She was afraid it was true that pride went before a fall, and she wasn't about to push her luck.

As it turned out, Rob pushed it for her by skating up beside her, exclaiming, "Hey, Mom! You're doing great!"

He didn't bump into her, but he did startle her. Caroline turned her head toward him with a silly smile pasted across her lips. Then she lost her balance. With a shriek of surprise she felt her feet scoot out in completely opposite directions, and she tumbled backward—right into Greg's arms.

"Oh!"

"Take it easy."

Her arms beat the air, and Greg gripped her, pulling her back against him.

"Gosh, Mom, I'm sorry," Rob put in, his eyes widening perceptibly as he took in the manner in which Greg was holding his mother. "I didn't mean to scare you."

"It's all right," she responded shakily. Seeing her son's speculative assessment, she plucked at Greg's hands and arms, which were firmly entrenched perilously high on her ribs. Greg didn't give an inch. A tentative move to stand on her own feet brought the undersides of her breasts into contact with the arms that held her. She quickly abandoned any attempts to escape and instead folded her arms across Greg's as though she might hide the source of her embarrassment. "Are you two—" She cleared her throat and tried to look parental. "Are you and Kim having a good time?"

"Terrific!" Rob declared with a dazzling grin. "We decided we couldn't risk the egg on the rink, so we've been sitting at the snack counter talking. I came over to, well, to tell you what a good job you were doing."

"Thanks," Caroline said dryly. From her shoulders to the back of her thighs, she was acutely aware of the heat and strength of Greg's body pressing into her. He held her as though she would collapse in a heap if he let go. And unfortunately the chances were excellent that she would. She could either deal with her son watching her being held closely by a man, or she could deal with falling. Her son, she decided, was forgiving. The floor was not.

"You know, Caroline," Greg began, "I'm ready for something to drink. How about you?"

"Oh, what a wonderful idea!" she exclaimed, her feet making diligent efforts to go in the proper direction. She hoped Greg would cooperate and help her to the side. And, bless his heart, he did. Only he never shifted his grip but simply proceeded to skate with her in front of him. He did it so well and so smoothly that it felt as though her body were merely a part of his. All the while he continued talking to Rob, who skated at their side, eyeing the arrangement with avid curiosity. Caroline feigned nonchalance.

When they reached the bench Greg finally released her. She sank down and lifted her eyes to meet his. A mischievous grin was spreading itself across his face. It made his eyes crinkle at the corners in a way Caroline found nearly irresistible.

"If you give me your skates, I'll take them back to the rental center for you. That is—" he winked "—if you think you can part with them."

"Give me a minute. I'll be ready for the next ten laps."

"You want to spend tomorrow plugged into a heating pad?"

"You think I'm gonna be sore, huh?"

"I think you're pretty wonderful, but I also think you ought to give me the skates."

Caroline looked around for Rob, but he had gone back to Kim. She tried to tell herself it shouldn't bother her to have a man flirting with her in front of her son. But it did bother her. It bothered her a lot. She hadn't maintained years of strict control over her behavior only to blow it now, when it counted the most.

It was tricky walking across the carpeted floor toward the snack counter on her own two feet—rather like walking on dry land after being on board a ship for a week, but Caroline made the journey without mishap. She sat with Rob and Kim until Greg came back from returning their skates. When he slid onto the stool next to her, she turned to Kim.

"Why don't you and Rob go skate for a while. I'll watch the egg for you."

"Oh, Ms. Forrester, that's all right. We're having a good time talking. I'm sorry I went off and left the egg before. I shouldn't have done that."

"Well, nothing happened this time," Caroline replied. "And I really don't mind egg-sitting for a while. Go on."

Kim looked at her father questioningly.

Greg smiled. "Go ahead, princess. Have a good time."

"All *right*! You're terrific, Mom!" Rob declared, planting a quick kiss on Caroline's cheek and then turning to Kim, who didn't waste any more time arguing.

"Like the boy said," Greg spoke quietly. "You're terrific."

Caroline turned to meet his gaze. Without thinking, she answered, "You're pretty terrific yourself. I had a wonderful time out on that rink, and I wouldn't even have tried if you hadn't insisted. Besides which, you kept your promise

not to let me make a fool of myself by falling on my...
backside." Her lips twitched in a tiny smile.

Greg's gray eyes were lit with humor. "You don't hate me
for pawing you like that in front of Rob?"

"I considered it," she admitted to him at the same time
she admitted to herself how nice it was being in the company of a man who understood what it was to be a parent.
She didn't have to tell him how she'd felt. He'd simply
known. The level of intimacy between them took another
leap forward, and Caroline couldn't bring herself to pull
back from it.

"My pride won out, though," she went on. "I decided I'd
rather have him think I was playing it fast and loose than
have him watch me splatter all over the floor."

"Smart choice," Greg said, chuckling.

Caroline wasn't so sure it was but chose not to think
about the reasons why. There would be plenty of time later
for second thoughts. The night was still young.

Three

As it turned out, the night was older than Caroline realized. They had to leave the rink at nine-thirty to allow Greg to get ready for a late flight to Los Angeles. She refused to acknowledge her disappointment over having to go home as being personally motivated and told herself she was sorry Kim and Rob had to cut their evening short.

It occurred to her as she was getting ready for bed that Greg must be away from home a lot. She didn't know much about the life of a commercial airline pilot, but she knew more than she had even wanted to know about the life of a woman whose husband is never home. It was empty and lonely, full of unfulfilled dreams, broken promises and hours of waiting. For her there had also been 2:00 a.m. feedings, piles of laundry, emergency trips to the doctor's office and days spent searching for reliable childcare. Always in the back of her mind, there'd been the questions— where was he and what was he doing?—but she had known the answers all too often. The knowledge had finally forced her to make a choice: she could get a divorce or lose whatever self-respect she might have left. Caroline chose the divorce.

As she stood in front of the bathroom mirror brushing her shoulder-length hair, she admitted that, besides the fact they were both away from home a lot, Chuck Forrester and Greg Lawton were completely dissimilar. Chuck would never have bothered to talk to Rob's teacher about his concerns, nor would he have gone out of his way to meet a girl Rob was interested in dating.

Most of all, though, Chuck lacked any of Greg's sensitivity or emotional maturity. The last time she'd spoken to him—a year ago, it had been now—her ex-husband hadn't behaved any differently than he had at nineteen. He still wore jeans that were too tight, and he still smelled like car grease and beer. He still treated Rob like a toy he'd never wanted but felt obligated to play with occasionally. Even the demise of his second marriage hadn't made him wise up to the fact that party time was over. Caroline doubted if anything ever would.

To compare Chuck to Greg was, to put it in terms Chuck would have understood, like comparing a battered pickup to a sleek sports car. Chuck wouldn't get off the starting line before Greg had won the race. And as a parent, Chuck wouldn't even qualify to start. Despite his erratic work schedule, Greg had obviously been a thousand times more of a father to Kim than Chuck ever would have been to Rob.

Still, from the point of view of the wife who had to stay at home and wait, absence was absence, whatever the reason.

She was in her bathrobe, turning out lights and locking up the house by eleven-thirty. Rob had gone to bed half an hour before, certain he was too excited to sleep. Caroline had to smile when she peeked in his door to find him sprawled across his bed, dead to the world. He had, as usual, forgotten to take off his Walkman. She crept into the room, carefully removed the earphones and turned off the radio. He might not care about his ears, but she did. Funny how much, and yet how little, had changed: when he had been a baby, she'd removed a pacifier from his mouth. At ten it was a baseball glove from his hand. It didn't seem odd to be removing a set of earphones now. It was all part of a ritual established years ago.

Caroline was on her way to bed when she heard the faint chime of the front doorbell.

Cautiously, wrapping her long robe more tightly around her middle, she descended the stairs and peered through the peephole. Greg was standing on her front step with the hat of his pilot's uniform tucked beneath his arm. She released the chain immediately and opened the door.

"Hi." He smiled lopsidedly.

"Is everything all right?" she asked, her gaze taking in his navy jacket with its gold buttons and captain's bars at the shoulders. His shirt was white, and he sported a red and blue tie. His sandy-colored hair, still a little damp from the shower, was combed neatly in place. He looked exceptionally handsome.

"Everything's fine," he replied, his gray eyes doing an appraisal of their own. Caroline was wearing a dark green terry cloth bathrobe, and the tips of her bare toes were peeping from beneath its hem. "I'm on my way to the airport, but I wanted to talk to you. I hoped you wouldn't be in bed yet."

Caroline's hand went automatically to her loose hair as she glanced down at her state of dress. "Well, actually, I—"

"I'll only keep you a minute. Please."

Her problem was that she'd always been a pushover, Caroline decided as she ushered Greg into her kitchen. He took her up on her offer of a cup of instant coffee and sat toying with the rim of his hat as she made it.

"Looks like you've got a resident artist," he remarked, glancing about the tiny kitchen at the various drawings that covered the walls. Some were done in pen and ink and others in watercolor. They all bore the signature "Rob" in the lower right-hand corner. "They're very good," Greg added thoughtfully.

Caroline tossed him a quick smile over her shoulder. "I'd agree with you, but you'd say I was prejudiced. When I bought the townhouse four years ago, I'd only been teaching two years, and I had to decorate it on a shoestring budget. It occurred to me that sixteen years worth of Rob's artwork was the perfect solution to bare walls. I matted my favorites, and, well, you see the results."

"Not a bad idea," Greg commented. Swinging around on his chair, he leaned forward to study the walls in the adjacent dining room. "There's a theme to a lot of his work, isn't there? Does he have an interest in a military career?"

"No," Caroline answered, turning the burner off under the whistling kettle of water. "Rob's a Civil War buff. There've been moments when I thought if I had to visit one more battlefield, I'd scream, but he never gets tired of it. He wants to go to Princeton or Yale and major in American history."

Greg turned back on his chair toward the kitchen table and laid his hat upon it. "Like I said, Caroline, you've got a fine son, one you can be proud of. To my knowledge Kim hasn't given a thought to life after high school."

"Give her time," Caroline urged as she set their coffee on the table and took the chair across from him.

The look he gave her was one that told her the conversation was about to get serious.

"Caroline," Greg began, then paused as though searching for words. "I want to thank you for everything you've done this past week for Kim and me.... No, that's not true. I want to thank you for what you've done for *me*."

"Oh, Greg, no—"

"Oh, Caroline, *yes*." He cut her off as he reached across the table for her hand, imprisoning it in his own as though it were the most natural thing in the world to do. "I can't possibly tell you what it's like to climb into the cockpit of a 727 to go flying off to Los Angeles, knowing I won't be back for two or three days and wondering what's going to go on while I'm gone. When Joanne got sick, I grew accustomed to worrying all the time. After she died, I transferred all that worry to Kim, and it's gotten worse as the years have gone by. When I met you last Friday, I'd about reached the end of my rope. I couldn't handle being faced with the fact that my daughter needed to know *all* the details about being a woman and a responsible adult."

He looked down at the hand holding Caroline's. His thumb rubbed absently at her wrist as a wave of some strong emotion swept across his face. "If you'd been anyone but who you are, this entire thing could've been a disaster. I could've made the biggest mistake of my career as a parent. And it's only because you *are* an incredibly sensitive, gentle woman that I've been able to see my own fears for what they are." His gaze lifted to meet hers once more.

Caroline stared at him, at a complete loss for words. She was touched by his vulnerability and his honesty. She was warmed and pleased by his words. And she was scared to death of the way he made her feel when he looked at her as though he'd like to wrap her up and take her home.

"Greg," she began in a voice made hoarse by her uncertainty, "I haven't really done anything. Kim is a wonderful girl. She didn't get to be one by accident. You've been a good father all along. I only gave you information when you needed it."

He shook his head. "You've done more than that. Last Friday, when I attacked you, you didn't get all self-righteous and defensive. A lot of teachers would have, but you listened and explained. And you never took the choice away from me. You supported *me* as a parent and as a person." His eyes took on an amused gleam. "And tonight. It was certainly above and beyond the call of duty for you to suffer through the roller rink scene. Don't think I don't know the reason that you came along was to keep the old man occupied while number-one-son made his move on the sweet-young-thing."

Caroline couldn't resist the smile that tugged at her lips. "Rob was a little put out when it finally hit him that he wasn't going to get to kiss Kim good-night, unless he wanted an unappreciative audience."

Greg threw back his head and laughed. "Judging from the look on my daughter's face when she went to bed, I'm pretty sure he'll get his chance."

"So I told him." She chuckled, too, then asked hesitantly, "Does this mean you're going to let them see each other again?"

Greg let go of her hand to spread his arms in surrender. "I'm outnumbered," he said. "I can barely resist Kim. How can I possibly resist Rob and you, too? Besides, I decided last Friday that any son of yours has got to be the best thing that could happen to my daughter."

Caroline felt herself blushing, and she looked down. "That's a very nice thing to say."

"It's true. And it's wonderful to have some peace of mind for the first time in years. That's what I'm trying to tell you. This past week I've felt like a new man. I flew to Dallas on Monday and to Chicago on Wednesday. I'm going out to L.A. tonight and won't be back until Sunday, but I'm not the least bit worried about anything. And that's a good thing, Caroline, because it's damned hard to worry when you're at thirty thousand feet, in control of a plane full of people whose lives are depending on you."

Caroline shivered a little as it sank in that he really meant what he was saying. He wasn't being merely polite. The support she'd given him, which had seemed such an insignificant thing to her, had truly made a difference in his life. A critical difference. His gratitude was real. And that, Caroline could accept. It was from one parent to another. One human being to another.

But there was something else that didn't have anything to do with gratitude or being a parent, something that was lurking in those gray eyes, turning them smoky and warm. She opened her mouth to talk, to keep him from naming the feeling that she sensed growing between them, but it was too late. He was speaking; and suddenly her heart speeded up, and her insides began to quiver.

"Now that I've made my little speech about how grateful I am and how wonderful I think our children are, I can get on to the real reason I'm here." He paused for an instant, his gaze searching hers intently, questioningly. "I want to see you again, Caroline. Without the kids. Will you go out to dinner with me next Tuesday?"

There it was. Oh, how she wanted to say yes! And oh, how hard it was going to be saying no.

But she had to. She'd dated over the years, but she'd dated men who didn't particularly excite her, men who were safe and more friends than lovers. The one time she'd broken this rule, the result had been disastrous; she had been disappointed, and Rob had been hurt by what appeared as yet another man's abandonment of him. Since that time, having determined she couldn't subject herself or her son to the emotional roller coaster love affairs often were, she'd dated only men who weren't likely to cause her a minute of lost sleep.

Intuitively, Caroline knew that Greg Lawton was a man who could cause her more pain than she'd ever before experienced. And that truly scared her. Even sitting in her old bathrobe at the kitchen table, even when he wasn't touching her in any way, his presence made her feel things that only one other man had ever made her feel. She hadn't said no to that man and her whole life since had been spent paying for the mistake. She didn't regret anything that had brought her Rob, but she had no intentions of making the same mistake twice. And saying yes to a date with Greg Lawton would be taking the first step toward doing precisely that.

"Greg, I..." Her voice faded, and a strained silence rose between them as she fumbled for an excuse that sounded plausible. "I can't."

His brows drew together for a moment. "Why? Am I mistaken in thinking that you enjoyed the evening as much as I did?"

She shook her head. "No, I had a wonderful time tonight. But I agreed to go because I wanted to help Rob, and I wanted to help you and Kim, too. But..." She paused. "I know I'm not Kim's teacher; yet I still think it would be very unprofessional of me to date the father of one of the students in my school. Times may have changed, but we don't live in the most liberal community where certain things are concerned." Caroline lifted her eyes to his for the first time since she'd begun her proper little speech. She hoped her expression was appropriately cool. She was certain it was properly regretful.

Greg, however, was not going to be satisfied with cool and regretful.

"Baloney," he said flatly. "That's the poorest excuse I've ever heard. Unfortunately—" he glanced at the wall clock and rose from the table "—I don't have time tonight for you to think up a better one. You'll have a couple of days to work on it. And you'd better make it good because I'm not planning to give up."

Caroline rose with him, shoving her hands down into the deep pockets of her robe. She steadied her lower lip between her teeth for a moment before saying, "I'm sorry, Greg. I'm not trying to be coy."

Greg shot her an infuriatingly patient look. "Caroline, you haven't got a coy bone anywhere in that lovely body." And with that he picked up his hat and began walking toward the front door.

Shakily, Caroline followed.

At the door he stopped and turned to her. "I want to see you again, and I can't think of a single reason why I shouldn't be able to. Unless there's someone else?"

She couldn't lie about it, and she answered his question with a little shake of her head.

"Or unless you're an amazingly good actress and really can't stand the sight of me?"

Again, she shook her head, this time with her gaze about level with his chest.

"I'm damned curious to know what you're thinking," he told her. "I wish I didn't have to go. I'd like to stay and have you tell me about this barrier I see you building between us." With a finger under her chin, he lifted her face to his, and his voice seemed to drop several octaves as he added, "At least, let me give you something to think about while

I'm gone. Lord knows, I've been thinking about it all night.''

Caroline knew what was coming and tried to pull away but found she couldn't. There was something irresistible about the way his eyes held hers as he lowered his head toward her. There was something even more irresistible about the way his lips touched hers so tenderly and with such promise. And he fulfilled the promise with his lips alone, drawing her to him, courting her, rocking gently across her pleasure-softened mouth with a finesse that made her breathless. And left her wanting.

"Good night, Caroline," she heard him say, his breath warming her cheek.

When her eyes opened halfway, she found she was alone. She blinked, her eyes widening as she saw Greg striding down her sidewalk. His shoulders were broad inside his blue jacket, and his step was light and confident.

She was shaking like a leaf, and her heart was racing wildly. Her hands were clenched into fists inside the pockets of her robe, and her eyes were filled with a soft wonder that was incredibly sensual but for a tiny spark of fear.

An intriguing puzzle. That's how Greg thought of Caroline as he drove to Dulles International Airport. There was more than one Caroline behind those big blue eyes; yes, a many-faceted creature dwelled within that soft, feminine form. A mature, incredibly confident woman on the one hand and a slightly awkward, blushing schoolgirl on the other. Alive with quick-witted humor one minute. Saddened, and maybe a little bitter, the next.

The expression on her face as he'd turned to leave her lingered in his mind. Purity, almost innocence, the likes of which he hadn't seen in years. Soft, melting arousal, too, and a sense of expectation that had said she wanted more. And more was what he very much wanted to give her.

There had been other women since Joanne's death. Not many, but enough so that he wasn't feeling raw and hungry and aching for a woman's—any woman's—attention. He'd had time to work through his grief and to think about his life and the future. When he'd stopped bewailing all the ways in which he'd been dealt a lousy hand, he'd started to count his trump cards. The first thing he'd realized was that his fifteen years of marriage to Joanne was the best thing he had going for him. He knew what a good marriage was and what was possible when two people loved one another well. And he wasn't about to settle for anything less. He did not, however, want to go through the rest of his life alone.

In that light the market narrowed considerably when it came to available women. Dating for the sake of dating was generally a waste of time. He found dating women twenty years younger than himself boring. Women who didn't want to be bothered with a teenage girl were out. And dating for the sake of sex...well, he'd done that upon more than one occasion, but it left a lot to be desired.

Caroline Forrester was the first woman in five years he'd felt drawn to in any but the most physical sense. And the attraction had been immediate. He'd known intuitively that *here* was a woman with whom he could share a strong, emotional bond as well as a lasting physical desire. And each time he'd seen her, his first impression had been reaffirmed.

Her refusal to go out with him puzzled him a little. There was a reticence about her that he didn't understand. It seemed so incongruous with her innately open, giving personality. Being a goal-directed, somewhat single-minded individual, Greg reasoned that, if the look on her face when he'd kissed her was any indication, her refusal would turn into an acceptance very soon. It had better. Because the memory of that kiss was going to haunt him all the way to the west coast and back.

By the following morning the tiny spark of fear Caroline felt when Greg kissed her had grown into a full-fledged blaze. She had gone to bed in a slightly dazzled fog, but all the vague reasons why she knew she must say no to Greg Lawton crystallized in her mind overnight. This man wasn't just threatening. He was fatal. He was like a beautifully gift-wrapped box of the richest chocolate money could buy, and Caroline had never been able to resist chocolate. She'd be out of her mind to think for one minute that she could ultimately resist Greg. In fact she wondered if she could live through even a single evening without simply melting at his feet in a puddle of too-long suppressed needs and desires. They'd wind up making love eventually, and she absolutely wasn't ready to let that happen. Her son's well-being and her own depended upon her ability to keep her carefully guarded feelings in their proper place a little while longer.

So, when Greg called her Sunday night and asked her again to go to dinner with him, she gave him a firm refusal.

There was a long moment of silence over the phone during which Caroline held her breath, waiting for the argument she knew Greg would give her. Perversely, a part of her wanted him to argue, wanted him to change her mind, but the larger part of her gathered its forces to do battle.

Greg's voice, when he spoke, was rough. Clearly he was making an effort to control some strong emotion, and Caroline wondered if it was anger or disappointment.

"I don't understand you, Caroline."

Carefully she replied, "There's nothing to understand, Greg. We had a pleasant evening with our children. I expect there will be other occasions when we'll see or talk to each other, if Kim and Rob continue to date. But I don't want to go out with you."

"Don't want to, or just plain won't?" he pushed.

"You're asking the same question," she countered. "I told you the other night, I'm in a sensitive position at work right now, and I can't afford to do anything that might be construed as questionable. It doesn't matter whether I *want* to go out with you. I *don't* want to jeopardize my job."

"This is absurd!" he growled. "You'd think I was a syndicate boss or some crooked politician. How the hell is going out with a middle-aged widower, who lives in a decent neighborhood and has a decent job, going to jeopardize your career?"

"You know very well I'm not casting doubt on your respectability," Caroline told him. "This doesn't have anything to do with where you live or what you do for a living. It has to do with the fact that you're the parent of a student who's taking a controversial course that *I* designed and that *I* fought to have implemented. It's called conflict of interest. Pure and simple."

"I don't buy that malarkey for one minute."

Neither did she. Rather than continue to defend a position she didn't think was defensible, Caroline returned, "That's unfortunate. I'm sorry if you don't like my reason but the answer stays the same."

There was another long silence. Caroline could almost hear Greg regrouping before trying his next tack.

His voice was different when he spoke, quiet and gently curious. "Caroline, won't you tell me what's wrong? Is it because I kissed you without asking? Did it frighten you? Or has somebody hurt you so badly that you're afraid of the feeling that seems to hang in the air every time we look at each other? Tell me. Please."

Caroline took a deep breath and tried to control the urge to cry, *Yes, I'm afraid! And, yes, I've been hurt. And I'm not going to let that feeling that we both know is there hurt me again!* His guesses were so close to home it was unnerving. The conversation had suddenly become very painful, and she sought to end it quickly.

"You've had the only explanation I can give you, Greg," she said quietly. "I'm flattered and appreciate your asking, but I'm not going out with you. And talking about it any more isn't going to change my mind."

"Caroline, I—"

"I'm sorry, Greg. Good night."

There was an interminable pause, and Caroline half expected further argument. But he only grumbled an angry, "Good night," and hung up.

Caroline went to work Monday morning telling herself she should be pleased for sticking to her guns and resisting temptation. Yet, she couldn't shake the feeling of despondency that settled over her. It had been a very long time since she'd allowed herself to contemplate an intimate relationship with a man. More than that, she had a deep-down feeling that Greg was a man whom she could truly care about in all respects, if she dared to let herself get to know him. And she resented the fact that he'd come along about two or three years too soon.

When she walked out of school that afternoon, she was depressed and irritable. Her plan was to stop and pick up some Chinese food for dinner and spend the rest of the evening indulging herself in inane TV shows. The stack of ungraded papers she had in her briefcase could wait.

The sight that greeted her in front of the school made her forget her bad mood, replacing it with puzzled concern. Rob and Kim were standing by one of the benches that were beneath the flagpole. Rob was talking heatedly. Kim was clutching egg number 1865's shoe box; she was crying.

"Is this a private fight?" Caroline asked, walking slowly up to the two young people.

"Oh, Ms. Forrester!" Kim gave her a startled look as the tears continued to stream down her face.

Rob dug his hands into his pockets and looked down at his sneakered toe, kicking the leg of the bench.

Caroline took in the scene then said, "I guess you don't want company, huh?"

Rob remained silent. Kim dropped her gaze to the egg and burst into another fit of crying. And it was then that Greg arrived to pick Kim up from school.

"Hi, gang," he said, startling Caroline as he walked up beside her. "Is the egg marriage in trouble already?"

Caroline's personal turmoil about him all faded in the light of the immediate crisis. Her frown, the little shake of her head and the shrug she gave him all indicated that something was wrong, but that she didn't know what it was.

"Oh, Daddy," Kim began, glancing from her father to Rob and then back at her egg. "It's awful, and we're not really fighting. Rob bought these tickets, you see, and we can't take the egg, but the tickets were *awful* expensive, and I really want to go. But he doesn't believe me. He thinks I'm being silly about the egg and all—"

"No, I don't," Rob put in, looking down at Kimberly, who raised tear-laden green eyes to his.

She sniffled a little. "You don't?"

"I told you that," he said with a frustrated sigh. "I'm just mad 'cause we both want to go and can't. I shouldn't have blown the money without asking you first. That's all."

Having gleaned the gist of the dilemma, Caroline cut in. "What are the tickets for?"

"The John Cougar concert at the Capital Center Friday night," Rob answered. "You know I've been wanting to go, Mom. I bought the tickets last week when—" he glanced at Greg briefly "—when it looked like Kim would be able to go with me. I wanted to surprise her."

"And I *was* surprised!" Kim put in. "I *do* want to go! Only we can't possibly take the egg to a rock concert. It's . . . it's just not the right environment, you know?" She turned pleading eyes to Caroline as though looking for support from another mother. "I realize it sounds stupid but, well, we're supposed to be thinking of this egg as a baby, right? And you'd *never* take a real baby to a rock concert! The poor thing might get traumatized for life or something!"

Caroline took a deep breath and congratulated herself on keeping a straight face. She heard Greg clear his throat but avoided looking at him, knowing they'd both be laughing if she did. Realizing Kim expected some support, Caroline drew herself together to comment.

"Your, uh, attitude is commendable, Kim. A rock concert is certainly no place for a baby. Don't you agree, Rob?"

Rob shrugged, obviously fed up with the whole thing. "I don't know about a baby, but I've gotta admit, taking the egg to see John Cougar would be certain death. It'd be scrambled before we ever got to our seats."

"Can't you take the tickets back?" Greg asked. "Or sell them to somebody else?"

Rob's jaw worked a little as he answered, "Sure."

"So," Greg reasoned, "Rob'll get his money back, and you two can go to some other concert after the egg project is over. Problem solved."

"They're disappointed," Caroline put in quickly, feeling that he was pushing the kids a little too hard.

"It's okay, Daddy," Kim said quietly. "John Cougar will probably be back next year. And if Rob can't sell the tickets or return them, I can split the cost—"

"No way," Rob cut in, folding his arms and spreading his feet in a determined stance. He wasn't too young to know what male arrogance looked like.

Kim, however, was too young to have learned the futility of arguing with such an attitude. "Don't be silly, Rob. Those tickets were expensive. You were trying to do something nice for me buying them, and it isn't your fault it didn't work out. I just wish . . ."

Her sentence hung unfinished, her expression of misery suddenly changing to one of restrained hopefulness. She glanced quickly at her father. "Daddy, are you going to be home Friday night?"

"Uh-oh," Greg mumbled. "Here it comes."

"Oh, Daddy, *please*!" Kim went on, the words tumbling over each other. "It'll be a whole year before John Cougar comes again, and I want to see him *now*. It's only one night and the egg's really no trouble. Honestly. All you'd have to do is sit it on the table and watch to make sure Tabby Cat doesn't bother it. I'd pay you double the going rate—that's four dollars an hour! And I'll never ask you to do it again. I *promise*!"

Greg started to say that two dollars an hour would be perfectly acceptable, but as he was about to give in, an intriguing idea flitted through his mind. It was sneaky. Caroline would probably hate him. But he was ready to use some dirty tactics. Especially if they worked.

"I'll do it on one condition," he said, and Kim immediately squealed with delight.

"I'll do anything, Daddy! Oh, thank you. You don't know—"

"I won't egg-sit alone."

Rob, who had been grinning broadly, stopped grinning. Kim looked confused. Then, slowly all eyes turned to Caroline, who felt the cold fingers of dread creep up her spine.

"Oh, no you don't, Greg Lawton," she began. "You're not going to get me to—"

"Why, Caroline!" Greg turned so that the kids missed the look he gave her. "This could work out great. I'll rent that movie you wanted to see, and we can watch it together while we, uh, sit with our little egg grandchild."

She was fuming. She was speechless. She couldn't say no, and he knew it.

In her mind Caroline ran through at least a dozen things she wanted to say to him, each one more vitriolic than the last. She hated being manipulated. She hated being out of control. But he'd trapped her, and she was going to have to swallow every last nasty thing she wanted to say. She didn't want the kids to know what had passed between their parents. That was the whole idea, wasn't it? To act as a model of responsible adulthood for Rob and Kim to follow.

"I'll do it," she bit out. "*This* time."

"Mom, you're terrific!"

Rob bounced over to hug her stiff form while Kim hugged her father and effused over what a wonderful father he truly was. All the while Greg's eyes remained locked with Caroline's behind their children's backs. And the message that passed between them was to the point.

Gotcha.

That's what you think.

Four

This is not a date. Caroline recited the words repeatedly as she got ready to go to Greg's house Friday night. To prove it, she pulled on her oldest pair of jeans, an oversize sweatshirt and a pair of sneakers. She didn't bother to repair her makeup from the day's wear, nor did she put her hair in its usual neat bun after she'd brushed it out but simply clipped it into a ponytail that bobbed about on the top of her head. Armed with a briefcase, three mysteries she'd been planning to read since last fall and a bottle of cherry soda, she was ready to go when Rob came bounding down the stairs.

"Gosh, Mom, we're going to be late!" he exclaimed, meeting her in the hallway. "I thought you were getting dressed."

Caroline eyed her son's apparel critically: faded denims tucked into heavy boots and a T-shirt with cut-out sleeves that prophesied, "The Good Die Young." Meeting his gaze, she cocked one brow. "I am dressed. What about you?"

He gave her clothes and "accessories" another once-over and shrugged. "Whatever turns you on. But I bet Mr. Lawton's gonna think you're strange."

Well, that was the whole idea, wasn't it? Caroline asked herself as she followed Rob to the car.

Once they'd arrived at the Lawton house, Rob couldn't have cared less what Caroline wore. His eyes were on Kim, who skipped excitedly out the door, wearing red stirrup pants with a matching top.

Greg, however, noticed Caroline's attire; it was clear that he, at least, understood the statement she was making. He turned to her with an amused look after the kids had left.

"Good evening, Ms. Forrester," he drawled lazily, closing the door. "You look lovely tonight. I especially like the cherry soda. Nice touch."

"Don't push your luck," Caroline shot back, taking in his khaki safari shorts and the pale pink, knit shirt he wore with them. "Keep in mind, we're egg-sitting. And that's it."

Greg chuckled. "Have you been preparing speeches all week to make me feel like a bigger heel than I already do?"

She frowned a little, confused by his almost sheepish look.

"I am sorry, Caroline," he said quietly. "I don't know what came over me Monday afternoon. I swear I'm not the impulsive type, but I wanted to see you badly and I guess I lost my head. Please. Forgive me."

Her frown deepened for a moment. Then, assuming a careless attitude, she remarked, "It's perfectly all right, Gregory. I don't mind egg-sitting. I, uh, had other plans for this evening, but this will give me a chance to get some work done. Next time, though, please consult me first."

His eyebrows lifted. *Gregory?* Where had that come from? It seemed that this sometimes confident, sometimes blushing lady could also pull off an act of cultured disdain when it suited her purposes.

Warily he told her, "I've made dinner for us. This is Mrs. Reid's weekend off, so it won't be fancy but you can consider it my peace offering."

"Oh, well," Caroline sighed, feigning indifference. "I'm not terribly hungry, but I suppose I will be later. I might as well eat when it's ready. And if you've gone to the trouble—"

"It was no trouble," he put in. Then, with a dubious glance at the things she carried, he added, "Why don't you put your briefcase and books in the study. I'll, uh, put the soda in the refrigerator."

Caroline agreed the study would be as good a place as any to work, and Greg left her, a disconcerted frown creasing his forehead.

With a sigh Caroline began to notice her surroundings. She'd had no idea Greg had such a spacious home. It was a modern house of wood and fieldstone with lots of windows. Ahead, through a double archway, was a formal living room. All the furnishings were in muted peach and sand tones, and there was a vase of fresh jonquils and Dutch irises on the mantle. Caroline guessed the house had been bought and decorated when Greg's wife was alive and they'd been planning a larger family.

Slowly she walked down the wide hall toward the study, finding it only a little smaller than the living room. It was paneled in oak with a hand-hewn mantle over a fieldstone fireplace. There was an oversize couch in front of a television set, two easy chairs and a desk with a home computer on it. On the walls were several huge photographs of airplanes in flight. Some were navy planes, and Caroline wondered if Greg had flown any of them himself.

She put her briefcase on the floor beside the couch and reviewed her simple game plan. This was not a date. She was here to help Greg watch the egg—however ridiculous that sounded—and she figured that wouldn't take up very much of her attention. She would spend the evening doing what she would have done if she'd stayed home alone. No matter what happened.

Dinner turned out to be an interesting event. In spite of his disclaimer that he'd gone to no trouble, Greg served her steak, baked potatoes and asparagus with cheese sauce, which they ate on trays in the study.

While Caroline applied herself to her food, Greg tried to draw her into conversation by asking her questions about her teaching, her likes and dislikes and her background. She replied with answers that were civil but hardly revealing. Yes, she liked her job. No, she had no plans to go into school administration. Yes, she'd gone to a local college.

Caroline didn't ask Greg anything, though it nearly killed her not to. She couldn't deny her curiosity about him any more than she could deny the effect he had on her senses.

He sat across from her, his bare legs stretched out on a buffalo-plaid ottoman, looking preposterously sexy in that darned pink shirt. A man should look feminine in pink, Caroline thought with a twinge of annoyance. His shoulders shouldn't look so broad, his bare forearms shouldn't look so strong. When he leaned back in his chair, she could see the outline of muscle across his chest. And his legs! They were long and powerful and covered with soft hair, sunbleached like the hair on his head. Did he go to Florida in the winter? Did he jog or play tennis? She sighed, doggedly attacking the last piece of steak on her plate. In pink or chartreuse, Greg was absolutely male. And she supposed she ought to be grateful he still had the TV tray on his lap; if pink shirts turned her on, what could a pair of safari shorts accomplish?

Greg accepted her offer of help with the dishwashing, which was fortunately a short-lived activity. Caroline was awestruck at first by the sheer size of Greg's kitchen; it was nearly as big as the entire downstairs of her townhouse. But the room shrunk to the size of a closet, it seemed, as they worked together. There was the accidental brush of his arm against her breast when he leaned around her to put the sour cream in the refrigerator, then the not-so-accidental bump of his hip against hers as he pushed her gently away from the sink. He gave her a very deliberate wink when she straightened from loading a pot into the dishwasher and caught him in the act of appreciating her denim-clad bottom. It was all much too intimate. Caroline knew her resolve was weakening and escaped from the kitchen, leaving Greg to clean the grill from the steaks.

Back in the study, she settled herself in a corner of the couch and pulled her briefcase onto her lap. She hoped that the sight of two hundred and fifty ungraded papers would serve as an effective mental cold shower. It was somewhat reassuring to discover that her libido was still so healthy, but she was determined that its urges would remain frustrated. She was not going to sacrifice everything she'd worked so hard to achieve for a few moments of passion.

When Greg entered the room a few minutes later, she had glasses perched on the end of her nose, a pile of papers in her lap and a red pen in her hand.

"Trying to find a place to put this egg that's safe from Tabby Cat is harder than you'd think. That damned animal gets into everything." Greg cast a disparaging glance at the well-fed feline, who was stretched out on the back of an easy chair, and walked to the mantel, where he carefully placed the shoe box out of harm's way.

Caroline glanced up warily, then her eyes widened. Kim had obviously succumbed to a moment of maternal instinct, for the box now sported a dust ruffle of bright yellow fabric with little brown teddy bears on it. At the head of the "crib" was a yellow satin bow. Caroline managed not to burst into laughter, but the back of her hand came up to cover her mouth, and she looked quickly back down at the paper before her.

She sensed Greg watching her as he stood by the mantel. A minute or so passed. Eventually, he strolled over and sat down beside her.

"Whatcha doing?"

"Grading papers."

"Hmph."

Caroline's eyes bored holes into Sarah Morton's labeled diagram of male reproductive organs. A minute passed before Greg spoke again.

"What's a *scrum*?"

Caroline turned her head to find him frowning down at the paper on her lap. When his gaze lifted to meet hers over the rim of her glasses, she blinked slowly. "What do you *think* it is?"

He shook his head. "Nothing I've ever heard of. Did I miss something?"

"She spelled it wrong."

"Oh...*Ohhh*!"

Caroline bit her lip to avoid giggling and returned her attention to the ungraded papers. Another brief silence ensued.

"You got many of those to grade?"

"About two hundred and fifty." Her red pen moved mechanically down the column of answers, circling those that were incorrect.

"Two hundred and fifty...hmph."

"Hmmm-mm."

Sarah Morton's paper got slapped face down on the coffee table with a C+ grade. Greg stared at the paper and then at the stack in her lap.

"You going to do all of them tonight?"

"Uh-uh." The pen circled three wrong answers in a row on the next diagram. "I won't get more than half finished."

"And you have to have them done Monday morning?"

"That's right."

"I see."

Caroline was certain he did see. She held her breath, waiting to hear him complain about her ignoring him. But he didn't complain. He only sighed. Then, much to her amazement, he got up, walked over to the TV and flipped it on. As an afterthought he turned to her.

"Will this bother you?"

She shook her head, and he picked up the remote control and brought it back to the couch with him. Flopping down beside her once more, he propped his feet on the coffee table and began to search for something to watch.

Thus passed the following two hours. They watched the last two innings of an Orioles game and the beginning of a PBS special about lions. Ten minutes into the show, Greg realized he'd already seen it and changed the channel. At ten o'clock he made popcorn, which sat in a big bowl on the coffee table and slowly disappeared, along with Caroline's cherry soda. Greg fell asleep somewhere in the middle of the eleven o'clock news.

Caroline looked over at him and sighed, feeling a little drowsy herself and oddly content. She removed her glasses and placed them beside the empty popcorn bowl. The papers went back into her briefcase as she listened to the weather report. When she pulled the clip out of her ponytail and leaned her head against the back of the couch, her intention was only to rest her eyes. She never meant to fall asleep.

The sound of gunfire woke them. Caroline frowned in her sleep, then blinked in confusion.

"What the hell?" a low, male voice rumbled close to her ear as she tried to lift her head.

"Ouch," she complained softly, her hand going automatically to find out what was pinning her hair. Her fingers encountered the stubble of beard on a masculine face. She pulled back quickly, unmindful of the slight pain from the caught strands of hair that she now realized were being held against the couch by Greg's arm. They'd both fallen asleep, gravitating toward the most comfortable spot, which turned out to be each other's shoulder. The noise that had awakened them was a rerun of an old war movie.

Caroline's head turned, and her eyes met Greg's.

He smiled lazily. "Guess we flunked the test."

With her brain still sleep-fogged Caroline stared at him, mesmerized by the tiny flecks of black in his gray eyes. Moistening her dry lips with the tip of her tongue, she whispered, "What test?"

He watched her unconsciously seductive action with fascination. "The egg-sitting test. First rule in the sitter's handbook. Don't fall asleep."

"Oh. I guess we did."

"We're going to flunk another one, too."

"Oh, no, which one?"

"Second rule. Sitters aren't allowed to make out. But I'm going to kiss you, Caroline. Right now."

It wasn't as though he hadn't warned her. Caroline simply didn't move to widen the gap between them. He didn't have far to go before his lips touched . . . tasted . . . and settled on hers. She was completely unprepared for the instant, almost convulsive fluttering inside her body that came when his mouth slanted, open and hot, over hers. Instinct took over. Her thighs pressed themselves together as her hand reached for his cheek, her fingers seeking to touch the source of the pleasure. Her parted lips trembled as his tongue entered her mouth to caress her. It was pure, mindless pleasure. Her senses were filled with him—the sound of his breathing, the smell of his skin, the feel of his unshaven jaw moving beneath her fingers as he kissed her.

He kissed her until she ached. Until she needed and wanted so badly that she was whimpering with the pain of not having. He kissed her until they were both gasping for breath, never quite ending the kiss before it began again. With that one endless kiss, he made her forget she'd ever been kissed before or by any other man.

And that was only the beginning. When his hands started moving over her, she went a little crazy. Her hips lifted against him, and in a husky voice she barely recognized as her own, she cried out, "Greg!"

"Caroline... Yes!"

The last vestiges of his control seemed to disappear at the sound of her calling his name. Suddenly his mouth was hungry. It sought to satisfy a need with whatever part of her it touched—the smoothness of her cheek, the whiteness of her throat, the bare skin of her shoulder, where it was exposed by the wide neck of her sweatshirt. His body pressed hers farther and farther into the deep cushions of the couch. And her fingers dug into his shoulders, her hands moving almost frantically across his back when his hand grazed lightly over her breast—then came back to linger there. The realization that he was shaking as he touched her only heightened her awareness that he was as caught in this storm of arousal as she. She arched, whispering his name.

"Oh, Lord, Caroline," he breathed. "You're so soft, so warm. You make me want so much."

His hand slid down over her ribs to the hem of her sweatshirt, and she had caught her breath in anticipation, when their lovemaking was brought to a gasping halt by the sound of a car door slamming closed.

"Damn!" Greg swore hoarsely.

For the very briefest moment—so brief it nearly could have passed unnoticed—his entire body collapsed against Caroline's. His fingertips touched the skin at her waist, and his lips brushed her neck, where her pulse was racing wildly. She felt the warm rush of his breath, felt his whole body tense as he nuzzled his cheek against her soft skin one last time.

Then, in the space of one breath, he was on his feet and reaching for Caroline's hand to pull her upright. Her free hand grabbed frantically at the bottom of her sweatshirt.

When Rob and Kim strolled into the room a few seconds later, their parents were sitting on opposite ends of the couch, guilt stamped plainly on their faces.

"Hi!" Rob greeted them brightly.

"Is the egg okay?" Kim asked, going immediately to the mantel to check on her baby.

"Junior's fine," Greg replied, his voice a little strained but remarkably well-modulated.

Caroline stared at the TV with unseeing eyes. Her cheeks were brushed with dots of high color, and her heart was still pounding against her chest. She'd never felt like a bigger fool in her entire life. She had to congratulate Greg, though. She doubted if she could have met Rob's eyes at that moment, but Greg was back in control and carrying on a conversation with the kids as though nothing cataclysmic had happened.

"How was the concert?"

"Oh, Daddy, it was wonderful!" Kim went on to give Greg an enthusiastic, if somewhat incomprehensible, description of the John Cougar concert.

Rob walked over to stand beside Caroline. Caroline sensed his eyes upon her and glanced up briefly. When she saw him frown in confusion, she knew he could tell something was not right. She forced herself to smile, though she wasn't sure he was reassured when he finally looked away.

Mercifully the evening ended soon after. Caroline managed to avoid Greg's watchful eyes until she and Rob were out the door. She didn't dare let herself think about what had happened until she was alone; but in the darkness of the car, she could feel the waves of heat wafting through her, whether from embarrassment or arousal she wasn't certain.

Later, standing before the bathroom mirror, Caroline stared at her reflection as though she were looking at a stranger. In spite of the anxiety Rob and Kim's sudden arrival had caused, her face still bore the signs of having been caught up in the throes of passion. Her eyes were luminous and wide, and she imagined what Greg must have seen when he looked at her. What had he thought then? Her mouth was rosy and soft and a little swollen; she wondered how it had felt to Greg when his lips had kissed it. And, oh, the man *did* know how to kiss. The memory rekindled the heat in her loins and she looked away, unable to meet her own gaze any longer.

She didn't blame Greg for what had happened. It had been the moment, the circumstances. Maybe if she hadn't fallen asleep, her guard would have remained intact. But maybes didn't count. Beyond any doubt, she knew that her power to resist temptation in the form of Greg Lawton had just suffered a serious setback.

Caroline couldn't feel guilty for getting sexually aroused by an attractive man who kissed like he'd made a detailed study of the art. She wasn't seventeen anymore, and she knew about sexual response. She understood what could happen when a person denied a need for physical fulfillment for long periods of time. And it had been a long time—too long. But it was going to have to be a little longer. When she finally did satisfy those suppressed sexual desires, it would be in a real relationship. One where she didn't have to be afraid of the consequences of losing control, where she loved the man with whom she was sharing her body and where she knew they'd have things to say to each other after the lovemaking was over. She wasn't interested in cheap thrills; what mattered to her was security and compatibility and constancy. And she doubted she would find those things with a man who was away from home nearly as much as he was there.

She liked Greg, knew him to be an intelligent man with a good sense of humor and an ability, that few men possessed, to admit his mistakes. The fact that he'd had a successful and long marriage that must have been fraught with problems made him all the more attractive. No, Caroline thought, it wouldn't be hard at all to fall head over heels in love with him. But the truth was they barely knew each other. It would have been foolish to think in such serious terms as falling in love when she had no idea if they wanted the same things from each other or whether their life goals were even close to being compatible. Maybe his tragic experience with his first wife had turned him against commitment forever. Maybe he was only interested in having a good time on a short-term basis. For pity's sake! Maybe he was grouchy in the morning and left dirty socks lying all over the house!

At that moment Caroline wasn't willing to take the risk that would be involved in discovering the answers to her questions. If she needed security, so did Rob, and he wouldn't find it with a mother who was caught up in the trauma of a love affair gone sour.

Greg called as she'd turned out her bedside lamp. She'd expected he would.

"I hope I didn't wake you up," he said when she answered the phone. "I had to call."

"I wasn't asleep," she replied.

He laughed, shortly. "I don't expect to get to sleep at all tonight. Caroline, I'm sorry. I know you were embarrassed. Hell! I was, too. I didn't mean to start something like that when I knew the kids would be coming home soon."

"It's not your fault," she told him quietly, cradling the phone against her shoulder and drawing her knees up under the covers. "I didn't exactly kick and scream, did I?"

He didn't answer the question, and his voice was low and rough as he spoke. "Caroline, I want you. I'm lying here *aching* with wanting you. Please, see me again. Give us a chance."

Her eyes closed. "Greg, I can't. I...I just can't."

"Why? Dammit, I'm not a fool. I know when a woman wants me as badly as I want her. And I know when a woman likes me, too. And you *do* want me and like me, Caroline. Why won't you admit that?"

"I'm not denying it," she replied. "On either count. But look at what almost happened. What do you think Rob and Kim would have thought if they'd actually found us..." She fumbled for words.

"Making love?" he supplied, then continued, "But they didn't find us. And if they had, it would have been embarrassing and awkward, maybe, but not shameful. *Are* you ashamed of being attracted to me, Caroline?"

"No, of course not," she denied, wondering if she were.

"Kim and Rob aren't babies," he added. "And they don't even need all the wonderful things you're teaching them in school to know that their parents are sexual beings, just like regular people.''

''But their parents aren't married,'' she put in before she could stop herself.

There was a silence on the other end of the phone. Caroline could hear the click as the numbers on her digital alarm clock flipped over to read 1:00 a.m.

Finally Greg spoke in a tone laden with disbelief, ''Are you trying to tell me that in this day and age and at your time in life, you hold yourself to that kind of standard?''

Caroline bristled defensively. ''That standard happens to be the one our society still uses when it judges a woman. I didn't make the rules, but I've had to live with them all my life. And whether I like it or not, I intend to measure up, if only for the sake of my job and my son.''

He sighed, and she could almost see him rubbing his hand across his face in frustration. Then he said, ''Caroline, I'm in no state to argue with you about this right now. Anything I say is going to come out sounding like I'm only interested in getting you into bed any way I can. And that's not true. Won't your... your code of ethics for proper behavior stretch to going out to dinner with me?''

It was such a reasonable request that Caroline almost gave in. It ought to be okay to see him. And only the knowledge that what lay between them would never end over a dinner table in a restaurant made her refuse.

''I can't, Greg. Please, don't ask me again.''

''Caroline—''

''I've got to go, now.''

''Caroline, dammit, don't you hang up!''

But she did. And then she lay staring up at the shadowed ceiling of her room. Never, in all the years of being a single parent, of putting herself through school, of facing classrooms full of hypercritical teenagers, had she felt so completely alone.

Greg slammed the phone down and flung himself back onto the bed. His body ached with unfulfilled arousal. His palms were damp. His heart hadn't stopped racing since Caroline had entered the house at six o'clock that evening. But he felt alive in a way he hadn't felt in years, and he'd be damned if he was going to give up now. Whether she knew it or not, Caroline Forrester, with her cute little ponytail and her bottle of cherry soda and her soft, womanly body had bought herself a one-way ticket on a very private flight. And it was up to him to make sure she got on the plane.

Five

It took considerable effort, but by Monday morning Caroline had nearly convinced herself that her uncustomary behavior in Greg's arms on Friday night was a matter of pure libidinal frustration. Thus categorized, she reasoned she had done the right thing in ending the relationship before it had really begun. She would be feeling better shortly—as soon as her body's chemistry had a chance to return to a normal level of activity.

It would have helped if she hadn't had to constantly hear about Greg. Rob, however, had taken to spending a good deal of time at the Lawton house and seemed to be almost as enamored of Greg as he was of Kim. Caroline was careful to hide her personal turmoil. She was honestly grateful for any time Rob could spend with an older man who might give him some of the attention he'd lacked from his father. After the divorce Chuck had seen Rob once a month. By the time Rob was in the sixth grade, the visits had become, at best, sporadic. At present they averaged about once a year, when Chuck would breeze through town, unannounced, on his way to a car race. She was frankly surprised that he bothered at all and sometimes wished he wouldn't. His visits only served to upset Rob, sometimes causing him to brood for days afterward over the unanswerable question of why his father didn't care about him.

Thus, when Rob told Caroline excitedly that Greg and Kim had invited him to spend the weekend at their beach cottage on the Outer Banks of North Carolina, she was genuinely delighted. Her delight turned to mild disappointment, though, when she discovered that Greg wouldn't be there. Kim's mother's parents, Faye and Larry Ferguson, were flying up from Florida to spend the weekend with the kids. Still, the fact that Greg had issued the invitation indicated he was willing to include Rob as part of the family. Caroline sent Rob off after school on Friday afternoon in Kim's shiny red Camaro with only a twinge of concern about the two of them driving all the way to North Carolina.

When the phone rang that night at nine o'clock, it didn't occur to her that it might signal trouble. The sound of Rob's voice came as a surprise.

"What's wrong?" she asked instantly.

"Nothing awful," he sighed, responding to her worried tone. "We got here a few minutes ago, and the phone was ringing. Mr. and Mrs. Ferguson aren't coming. Something about a neighbor getting sick and needing their help. They said they tried to call Kim before she left home, but they missed her. We can't call Mr. Lawton 'cause he's out of town, but we're afraid Kim will get in trouble if he finds out we stayed here alone. I don't know what to do. We're both pretty tired, and neither of us feels like driving all the way home tonight."

Caroline frowned. She didn't want them driving home, either—not after spending a full day at school and five hours in the car. On the other hand, she appreciated the children's concern that Greg might lose his newfound peace of mind if he discovered that his daughter had spent the night alone with Rob. For that matter she wasn't all that keen on the idea herself.

"How much money have you got?" she asked, searching for a solution.

"About forty dollars between us and Kim's gas credit card," Rob answered.

"Can you leave Kim at the house and go stay in a motel?"

"I thought of that," he admitted, "but Kim doesn't want to stay alone, and I don't blame her. This is really the end of the earth! And the people who own the only other cottage along this stretch of beach aren't here. Mom, I was thinking—" He hesitated. "Can you come down? I know it's a lot to ask, but I don't know what else to do. Besides, it's a great place. You could stay the weekend and have a vacation, too."

Caroline's first reaction was to say no. Then, on second thought, the idea seemed rather appealing. It made her a little nervous that it was Greg's house in which she'd be staying, but he wouldn't be at home. And it was certainly true that she hadn't had a vacation in a long time. The money simply was never there.

"Put Kim on the phone," she said. "I'll need directions."

"All *right*!" she heard her son shout. And she mouthed the words along with him as he added the obligatory, "Mom, you're terrific!"

Five and a half hours later, feeling anything but terrific, Caroline turned her car into the sandy driveway of the beach cottage. She was exhausted and completely disoriented. It seemed impossible that she'd actually left the city behind and was now on the northern finger of North Carolina's Outer Banks. As she turned off the ignition, she gave herself and Kim a pat on the back. The girl's directions had been excellent, or she never would have gotten there at all.

To say the cottage was isolated was an understatement. Desolate was more like it. No wonder Kim hadn't wanted to be left alone. The house was located north of the tiny village of Corolla where a one-lane road stopped. There was a dirt road as far as Greg's cottage, but beyond it nothing disturbed the endless line of sand dunes. While Caroline stared at the dark Atlantic Ocean, the screen door opened and Rob came out, looking sleepy and disheveled.

"Kim went to bed a long time ago," he told his mother, taking her suitcase out of the back seat. As they walked toward the weathered, gray-shingled cottage, he added, "You can stay in Mr. Lawton's room. Kim said he wouldn't mind."

Caroline minded but she didn't say so. It would look pretty silly for her to insist upon sleeping on the couch when there was a bed available—and a huge one at that, she noted, following Rob into the master bedroom. The house was an old one, he explained, which had been moved in 1936 from the dunes overlooking Currituck Sound to the oceanfront. Bare wood floors were strewn with an assortment of rag rugs; ships' lanterns wired for electricity were mounted on the walls and sand dollar wind chimes hung by the open bedroom window.

Rob shuffled off to bed, and Caroline was left alone to get settled. It was a good thing she was exhausted from the drive, she thought as she put on her nightgown, or it might have bothered her to climb beneath the sheets of Greg's brass bed wondering when he'd last slept there himself.

Wondering what it would be like to lie there with him, with the ocean sounds coming in through the open window and the moon filtering through the light curtains. Wondering what it would be like to make love with him until the sun came up over the watery horizon. Caroline's wonderings kept her awake for a very long time.

The next morning Caroline opened her eyes to find Greg lying beside her. The white shirt of his uniform was open halfway, revealing golden-blond hair sprinkled liberally across a muscular chest. His shoes were off. He looked tired and a little haggard, but his smile was warm as he lay propped on an elbow looking down at her.

She blinked in startled confusion and grabbed for the sheet, which was bunched around her waist. "Greg!" she croaked. "What are you doing here? Where are Rob and Kim?"

His hand reached up and smoothed her wispy bangs away from her eyes. "Don't get yourself all in a dither, Caroline. The kids are on the beach. And honest, when I walked in and found you like this, I couldn't help myself. Do you have any idea how pretty you are?"

She flushed and said weakly, "I thought you were out of town."

"I got home late and found a note from Mrs. Reid," he explained, his eyes moving slowly over her sleep-softened features and the halo of warm brown hair that lay across the pillow. "The note said Faye and Larry weren't going to make it this weekend. I tried to call you but you weren't home. I thought I'd better...come down and...and check...." He trailed off, his eyes drifting downward over the feminine curves beneath the sheet. His voice was a little hoarse when his gaze flashed back to hers. "I drove down as fast as I... Oh, Caroline, it's happening to me again.

Every time I see you, I get this feeling that I've got to kiss you hello, or the day just hasn't started.''

His kiss wasn't like any greeting Caroline had ever experienced. It was more like an explosion. Her head reeled as he fused his mouth to hers. And as she felt herself being pressed into the mattress by his weight, Caroline knew nothing she'd ever experienced had felt so good. Somewhat dazedly she wondered how long it would take her to become addicted to Greg's version of a morning greeting. And that thought sent a bolt of panic racing through her. With a muffled groan Greg shoved himself away and lay on his back with one hand clenched at his side, the other wrapped around a spindle of the brass headboard. Caroline peered cautiously in his direction, noting the rapid rise and fall of his chest and the drawn lines at the corner of his mouth. He looked so confused, so distraught—as if he were experiencing the same emotions that were, at that moment, warring within her own body. She turned away from him and, clutching the sheet above her breasts, stared out the window.

Outside a gull cried on the wind, two young people laughed in the distance and the ocean continued to crash, wave upon wave, at the shoreline.

Greg spoke quietly into the painful silence. "I think I've lost my mind. I haven't had this little control since ... God, I can't remember. I've got to get out of here." And with that, he shoved himself off the bed and left the room.

Caroline met him in the large common room twenty minutes later. He was standing by the galley kitchen drinking a glass of orange juice. He turned at the sound of her footsteps.

"Greg, I'm going home," she announced. "Now that you're here, the kids don't need me."

"No," he shook his head. "Stay. Please. It's a long drive to make for nothing."

"I don't think I should—"

"Besides, the kids would think it pretty strange if you suddenly picked up and left when I arrived. Do you want to have to explain it?"

No, she didn't. And he was right, it would look odd. Not that she'd thought of that in her hurry to pack and get away.

Caroline drew a deep breath. "I'll move my things out here and sleep on the couch," she said, starting hesitantly toward the grouping of couches and odd-sized chairs. The furniture was arranged before a series of French doors that ran the length of the room and overlooked the beach.

"You take that bag back to the bedroom," Greg ordered, clearly affronted. "I'll be perfectly fine on the blue couch. It opens up. I'll just get some things out of my room, then I won't have to . . . to go in there again."

Their eyes met briefly.

"I think I'll join the kids on the beach," Caroline said with a distinct lack of enthusiasm.

"Fine," he muttered, rubbing his hand over his face. "I'm going to catch some sleep."

Caroline changed into her bathing suit with some trepidation. When she'd packed the night before, she'd thought she was going to a deserted stretch of beach with only Kim and Rob. The bathing suit she'd brought along was one she kept for sunbathing in her tiny backyard with its high fence. It was not a bathing suit intended for public consumption—although Rob had thought otherwise when he'd bought it for her, after she'd saved enough money for them to join the community pool.

"Good grief, Mom!" he'd exclaimed, gaping as she modeled the suit for him. "Who'd of believed you'd look like something out of *Sports Illustrated*'s swimsuit issue!"

Then and there, Caroline had decided the only place the suit would ever get wet was in a sink full of Woolite.

The jet black maillot was cut high on the thighs and plunged in a daring V all the way to her navel. A single gold chain between her breasts held it tenuously in place. The back was low enough to show the dimples below her waist. Viewing herself in the full-length mirror that hung on the bedroom door, Caroline congratulated herself on being able to carry off such a creation at the age of thirty-five. She was a little sorry she didn't have the nerve to go public, wearing what amounted to a bikini bottom with suspenders.

With a sigh, she pulled a lemon-yellow, cotton tunic over the suit and picked up a towel. When she passed through the kitchen on the way to the beach, she caught a glimpse of Greg. He was already sprawled out, fast asleep, on the sofa. Feeling she would probably be safe for at least a couple of hours, she walked down to the beach.

The area Rob and Kim had staked out was marked by a blanket and a rainbow-colored umbrella, stuck down into the sand. Under the umbrella sat egg number 1865 in its dust-ruffled bassinet. A piece of white netting covered it— to keep the bugs out? Caroline wondered. Someday Rob and Kim would look back on this and laugh. And someday they would make good parents. Hopefully that day was far in the future, and more than likely they wouldn't see it together.

She spread her towel on the sand at a discreet distance from theirs. Then, pulling off her tunic, she began spreading a mild sunscreen over her exposed skin. She noted that Rob and Kim, in their efforts to use Kim's surfboard, had drifted a good ways down the beach. They were sitting on the board in the water, facing each other; and as she watched, Rob leaned forward to kiss Kim.

Caroline started to look away, feeling like an intruder. But then she frowned as she noticed the kiss wasn't ending. In fact it obviously was becoming quite heated. Her eyes widened when she noted exactly *how* heated.

For the first time she wondered if maybe she had been a little too casual about her son's relationship with this beautiful, young girl. She'd never had any reason not to trust Rob, but then he'd never been in love. Was he in love now? Was Kim in love with him? Would it all end as Greg had feared in the beginning?

She glanced across the sand, and her eyes fastened on the decorated shoe box. It was only an experiment, wasn't it? These kids didn't really take it seriously, did they? Surely they understood that it was only a school project.

Her eyes coasted out over the water again, and she was relieved to find that Rob and Kim were paddling toward shore. Kim was laughing, and they both looked quite young and quite innocent. Well, maybe not as innocent as they'd looked ten minutes ago. With a sigh Caroline decided she was being paranoid. It was probably a case of her own frustration projecting itself onto the kids.

When Kim and Rob came running up the beach toward her, she greeted them with the news that Greg had arrived and was asleep on the couch. Both young people were notably relieved they'd had the foresight to call her the night before. Kim went over to plop down on her blanket and, a moment later, called out to Rob, who had lingered with Caroline.

"Rob, come here and tell me if you think Jeb Stuart feels too warm. I don't think the thermometer is working."

"Be right there!" he answered, then turned back to his mother. "She worries about him all the time. You'd think he was a real baby, or something."

Caroline cocked one brow and grinned. "Jeb Stuart? She's given it a name?"

Rob shrugged. "Well, not exactly. That was my idea. You know. The Confederate general, James Ewell Brown Stuart. Jeb for short. It was a natural, his number being 1865 and all. Gotta go." And he took off toward his own blanket.

Caroline laughed softly. The studies done about the egg experiment had said that things like this would happen. The students involved often anthropomorphized the egg by giving it a name, worrying whether it had a rash or a fever and otherwise treating it as thought it were, indeed, a live baby. Two of her more radical students had glued a safety pin onto their egg, given it a pink Mohawk wig and named it Punky. Kim and Rob's reactions were all within the range of normal, and she didn't need to be worried. Still, it was a shock to actually see it happening to her own son.

Stretching out on her towel, Caroline prepared to enjoy a rare day of total relaxation. The breeze kept her cool, and the sound of the waves lulled her into a state of blissful contentment. She fell asleep under the warm, late April sun.

When she awakened, she was lying on her stomach. She rolled to her side slowly, stopping short at the sight of Greg stretched out a few feet away. The all-American beach boy had on tropical patterned bathing trunks and was leaning back on both elbows, gazing out at the ocean. His hair was slicked back, and his skin glistened with water droplets from a recent swim.

"This is getting to be a real habit," she muttered.

He looked up at her and grinned. "Waking up beside me?"

"Hmm." Caroline rolled the rest of the way to her back, then, realizing that she was close to being naked, sat up and reached hastily for the tunic.

"Don't bother," he said casually. "When I got here, you were on your back. I looked as much as I could stand looking. Then I went for a long, *cold* swim. That's some bathing suit you've got there, Caroline.''

Caroline eyed him as though she thought he might jump her at any moment. Then, deciding it would be prudent to prepare for such an event, she pulled on the tunic.

Greg sighed. ''All right, but don't blame me for ruining your tan.''

''Where are the kids?'' she asked, swiping at her bangs with her hand.

''Gone to a movie in town. They left about half an hour ago.''

''Oh. Did they take Jeb Stuart with them?''

He blinked slowly. ''Who?''

She grinned. ''The egg. Rob named it after one of his Civil War heroes.''

Greg's laugh was rich and full. ''Yes, they took Jeb Stuart with them. Next they'll be looking for godparents and wanting to have him christened!''

''I draw the line at starting a savings account for Jeb's college education.''

''We've got wonderful children, Caroline.'' Greg's laughter had turned into a warm, intimate smile.

''Yes, we do,'' she agreed, returning his smile, content to share that moment with him of pride in their separate accomplishments.

Then, with a slight hesitation, she gave in to the desire to know more about him. ''Do you ever wish you'd had other children?'' she asked. ''Kim is so bright, so full of life. I know how it feels to have a child like that and wonder what the next one would have been like.''

He nodded. ''It would have been nice to have had more children. We bought the big house with that plan in mind, but Joanne and I wanted to space our family. Partly because of my being away so much—my schedule was a lot worse when Kim was little—and partly because we were enjoying Kim and didn't want to push it."

He looked back out at the ocean, pausing a moment before continuing. "Then Joanne got leukemia. At first when something like that happens, you don't believe it. But it hit her hard, and we had to face the fact that she was going to die. There was little I could do—that *anyone* could do—to make things easier for her. I felt I did my part by taking permanent measures to see to it that she wouldn't get pregnant—which could have been dangerous for both her and the baby. She tried like mad to convince me not to have the surgery." He sighed, remembering. "She cried for days after I'd had it done, saying I'd probably want to get married again after she was dead—and how bad she felt that I'd never be able to have more children. But it doesn't work like that, Caroline." His jaw tightened perceptibly. "When you love someone, you're not thinking about the next person you might love. I was interested in keeping Joanne alive as long as possible. It turned out that she had remissions off and on for six years before the disease took her. Kim and I both have a lot of good years to remember, and I don't regret anything I did to make sure they happened."

He hadn't been speaking with any great emotion; the pain of his wife's death was an old wound, and time had healed what could be healed. Still, when he fell silent, Caroline studied his profile and wondered what it had been like for him when it was happening. Had he raged against the injustice of it? Was he the sort of man who cried? She thought he probably was. This man knew how to love, Caroline realized as she watched him. "Till death do us part" meant something to him that she couldn't yet begin to fathom. A part of her wanted to reach out to him, to somehow touch the scars that life had given him and perhaps make them less.

What would it be like to know that, no matter what happened, the man she loved would go on loving her until his or her dying breath? What would it be like to have *this* man love her that way? She didn't dare contemplate the question seriously. Knowing about Greg's marriage made him even more attractive to her—if that were possible—than he had been before. She wanted that sort of marriage for herself. She wanted...

"How about you? Do you ever wish Rob had a brother or sister?"

His question caught her off guard, and Caroline's mouth twisted in a wry smile at the irony of her thoughts. "Yes, I would have liked to have had other children. At least, at one time I would. That was before I discovered I would be raising them all alone."

Greg frowned. "How long have you been divorced?"

"Twelve years."

His frown became puzzled as he tried to compute the mathematics of what she was saying.

Caroline hedged for a moment, then decided that his own honesty deserved to be answered in kind. "I was seventeen when I got pregnant, Greg. I'd been married six months when Rob was born."

He stared at her for a moment. Then, quietly, he said, "Is that the reason why you're so interested in teaching young people the consequences of their sexuality?"

She held his gaze, but she didn't need to answer for him to know it was true. Instead, she explained, "I grew up in western Maryland in a little town near the West Virginia border. My parents were very religious. Or rather, they used their religion as an excuse for their rigidity. I never went out on dates. I wasn't allowed to talk to boys on the phone or have them over to the house. Sex was the work of the devil, and at seventeen I was totally ignorant about any aspect of it. The day I—'' She glanced away, momentarily embarrassed but determined now to make him understand. ''The day I got my first period, I was twelve. I had no idea what was happening to me, and it scared me to death. I thought I must be dying. My mother cried. She told me I was cursed like every other woman alive, and that's what I could expect for having sinful thoughts—not that I really knew what a sinful thought was.''

''Good Lord,'' Greg breathed, unable to hide his anger or his revulsion at such a state of affairs.

Caroline sighed. ''I was allowed to go to church social events. That's where I met Chuck Forrester, at the annual choir picnic. And I continued to see him on other occasions—mostly in church on Sundays. He was very handsome and charming in a rough sort of way. And he always paid attention to me, made me feel special. One Sunday evening he asked if he could take me home from choir practice. I said no, of course not, he knew my father would be coming for me at nine-thirty. But I let him talk me into going to the drugstore for a soda. The choir had been preparing music for the Christmas service, and the director had already gone over our parts. Chuck convinced me we had plenty of time to get back before anyone knew we were gone. I went with him because—'' Caroline hesitated, then went on almost defiantly ''—because I couldn't stand it anymore. I was sick to death of being an outsider. I wanted to be like the other girls. And when Chuck didn't take me to the drugstore at all but drove to Lookout Rock and parked, I didn't ask why. I was scared. But I was excited, too. And he . . . he made me more excited. When he started to make love to me, I hadn't the foggiest notion what he was doing, but it made me feel—'' she frowned a little as she searched for the word ''—loved, I suppose. I knew I shouldn't be allowing him to do the things he did, but I couldn't make myself stop him. And by the time it was over and I knew that what I'd done was very serious indeed, it was too late."

"You were pregnant," Greg concluded.

"End of story," she shrugged.

"No, only the beginning," he corrected. "So, Chuck Forrester married you."

She nodded. "He didn't want to, but he felt obligated. So did his parents, I think. Which, at the time, was a good thing because my parents kicked me out of the house. My father never spoke to me afterward."

"He's dead now?"

"He died ten years ago. My mother writes occasionally. When Rob was nine, she started sending him little things for Christmas. I've asked her if she'd like to come and visit, but she's refused every time. And she's never asked us to come see her. Acknowledging that Rob exists is as far as she'll ever go, probably. Forgive me if it sounds callous, but I don't much care at this point."

"What happened with your ex-husband?" Greg asked. "I gather it was a case of not being enough in love to work it out?"

"Of not being in love at all," she amended. "His sense of duty began and ended with financial support. I spent six years trying very hard to make the marriage work. I didn't love him any more than he loved me, but I did love Rob. I wanted him to have two parents and a home, and I was willing to *try* to love Chuck for Rob's sake. Chuck couldn't bring himself to reciprocate. He didn't want to be a father or a husband and could never accept the fact that he was both. At first he took a job in an auto repair shop. Then he got involved with another local boy named Denny who was going to drive on the race circuit. Well, the only thing Chuck ever really cared about was fast cars. He started going with Denny on trips, and before long he was gone nearly all the time. He lost his job, but he won enough races to make up for it. And being the naive thing that I was, I figured he was out there working hard. It took me a long time to realize that he could have been home a lot more, but he had *reasons*, other than car races, that made being away from home so appealing.''

Her meaning was clear, and Greg snorted his derision at a man who would be unfaithful to his wife, whether he loved her or not, while she was at home taking care of his child. ''Life hasn't been much fun for you, has it, Caroline?'' he said.

''Actually,'' she began, thoughtfully, ''the last twelve years haven't been bad at all. It was hellish putting myself through college, while I held down a full-time job and worried about whether Rob was getting the right kind of attention from the sitters I hired. But taking care of myself and him like that was infinitely better than staying in a loveless marriage where I had no integrity. Chuck was relieved to be free, and I haven't ever had to worry about him sending child support on schedule. And since I began teaching at Martha Custis, things have been very good. I'm happy with what I do. I'm pleased with my son. And it still feels like I have much too much time on my hands, now that I'm not working and going to school simultaneously.''

''Time to learn how to play,'' Greg smiled, and when Caroline gave him a quizzical look, he added, ''Roller-skating, for instance. It was harder for you than anyone realized, wasn't it? Acting like you were having a good time when you were scared to death.''

As it always seemed to do, his sensitivity and perception touched her deeply. It almost made her want to cry to have someone voice the feelings that she was so accustomed to keeping inside.

"I had a wonderful time that night," she told him honestly. "I may not know how to play, and I may still be a little scared of learning. But I'm not seventeen or twenty-three anymore. I've proven to myself by now that I don't have to be a victim of my parents' misguided child rearing practices. I've learned that God isn't the vengeful, unforgiving creature my parents made Him out to be. And I've found out that I can do anything I need to do in order to survive. I'm quite ready to learn how to play, even if I am getting a late start."

She met his gaze with a smile on her face; but the smile faded as she read the question in his eyes. If she were ready to learn to play, to enjoy life, why was she holding back from a relationship with him?

This time, however, Greg was beginning to understand why Caroline might be afraid of the deepening attraction between them—an attraction that was as much one of kindred spirits as of physical chemistry. It was such a powerful thing that it seemed as though he could have reached out and touched it. It shocked him a little to realize that he hadn't felt anything so compelling in years. Maybe ever. He was certain, though, that if he could get Caroline past her fears, it would be good for her to experience love as he was starting to believe they could make it together.

A sudden thought brought his ruminations to a stop. He wondered how long it had been since she'd been intimate with a man. Surely there must have been someone in all the time since her divorce. A worried frown appeared on his brow. Her responses to his lovemaking had been almost violent. He'd felt that way, too; but now he wondered if her reaction was more than simply a response to him. It had been a very long time since he'd made love to a woman who wasn't as experienced, or nearly as experienced, as himself. Was Caroline's response that of a thirty-five year old woman who hadn't been sexually involved in twelve years? Judging from what she'd said of her husband, it could have been even longer. The thought was a sobering one.

As the day wore on, Caroline found it harder and harder to maintain any degree of distance from Greg either physically or emotionally. Their talk hadn't helped matters. Not only had she learned enough about him to make her want to learn more, she'd told him things she'd told very few other people. Sally knew. Her friends in West Virginia, Meg and Tom Roberts, knew some of it because they'd been there when it had happened. But she wanted to tell Greg everything. She wanted to share herself with him more completely than she'd ever shared herself with anyone.

The terrifying possibility that she had fallen in love with him occurred to her somewhere around dinnertime on Saturday, and it made her almost crazy. If she could barely control her responses to him when they were based on simple lust, how was she going to control them if they were based on love?

In a frantic effort to avoid the entire issue, Caroline threw herself into group activities with the kids. Rob and Kim were gracious when she invited herself to go with them for pizza at six o'clock. And they didn't complain at seven-thirty when Caroline found the Trivial Pursuit game and suggested they all play—though Rob did give her a look of strained patience. But at ten, when Kim asked Rob to go for a walk on the beach, both of them made it clear that they didn't want company. Greg agreed to watch Jeb Stuart in exchange for a car wash and waved them out the door without a second thought.

Caroline stood before one of the French doors with her arms folded around her middle. There was a full moon rising over the water, and she watched as the two youthful silhouettes disappeared down the beach into a mantle of pearly-white light. There was a worried frown on her brow when Greg came up to stand beside her.

"Do you think it's smart to let them go off like that?" she asked.

He looked at her, mildly surprised. "They're only going for a walk, Caroline. The beach is safe."

"And empty. And dark."

"And you think they're up to something they shouldn't be up to."

"Don't you wonder?"

"Nope. I haven't given it a thought for days."

She turned her head to stare at him. "You certainly have done an about-face. When I encouraged you to ease up on Kim, I didn't mean you should forget that she's young and...and susceptible."

"Oh, Caroline," he sighed, turning her into his arms, ignoring her stiff resistance.

"Greg, no..."

"Relax," he soothed. "I'm not going to do anything but hold you and maybe kiss you a little. That's not so bad, is it?"

"But I don't want you to hold me or kiss me at all!" she cried, her frustration getting the better of her.

"Honey, that's just plain nonsense and you and I both know it."

"Please, don't call me that," she pleaded weakly, trying to avoid the tiny kisses he was planting all over her face and succeeding only in giving him more access.

"Don't call you honey?" he queried gently. "Why not? It fits, you know. Sweet and melty. Bright like sunshine. A little exotic, but mostly normal as rain. Has anybody ever called you honey before?"

She rested her forehead against his chin and whispered, "Nobody's ever called me anything but Caroline."

"Not sweetheart or darling, either?"

She shook her head a little.

His hand came up and lifted her face toward his once more. "Don't you think it's about time? I'd like to call you all those things. I'd like to tell you how sweet you taste when I kiss you and how good it feels to hold you. How long has it been since a man's held you, Caroline? How long has it been since you've let yourself be loved?"

Caroline lowered her forehead to his chin once more, her hands coming up to rest on his ribs. She honestly didn't think he'd believe her, even if she'd wanted him to know, and so she didn't answer.

He didn't demand a response. Tucking a fallen strand of hair behind her ear, he asked, "Why won't you let me make love to you, Caroline? Is it because you're afraid of how it feels between us? Are you worried about the same thing happening that happened when you were seventeen? It won't, you know. I *can't* make you pregnant. And you're not seventeen anymore. We're both grown-up people with lots of common sense. There's no reason for us not to enjoy each other. Not one."

"Yes, there is!" Suddenly Caroline's hands clenched into fists that she brought down on his shoulders. Then, pushing herself away from him, she took three paces toward the middle of the room and stopped, pressing a hand to her eyes in an effort to control the storm of emotion inside her.

But her control broke. "Don't you see, Greg?" she exploded as she began pacing back and forth in front of him. "There are at least two excellent reasons: our children! I don't know how you manage your life, but I absolutely will not have an affair in front of my sixteen-year-old son. You want to know how long it's been since I've been seriously involved with a man? The last time was when Rob was eight. I thought maybe I could love Steve Barton. I thought it would be okay to be with him because at twenty-seven, I couldn't possibly get hurt the way I had when I was seventeen. Well, I was lucky. I didn't get hurt. But Rob did. He thought he was going to get a father, and when Steve and I finally realized we were hopelessly incompatible, Rob was the one who suffered. I was disappointed, but I wasn't destroyed. And I realized I couldn't let my attempts to fill my needs destroy Rob. He was—and is—far more vulnerable than I.'' Caroline stopped pacing and turned to face Greg. He was frowning—but he was listening.

She continued. ''I divorced Chuck because I didn't want Rob to grow up thinking that all men cheated on their wives or that women naturally allowed themselves to be victimized by that kind of behavior. I *did* want him to grow up believing that sex and love went together and that having sex with somebody you don't love can hurt both of you badly. I want him to *think* about what he's doing. I want him to consider the consequences his actions could have, not only for himself but for any woman with whom he's involved.''

She spread her arms wide in a helpless, almost frantic gesture. ''What do you want me to do, Greg? You think it's time I let someone love me. Don't you think I know that? Don't you think I want that, too? Don't you think it's driving me *insane* to be around you and wonder what it would be like to make love with you? But the fact is, it's *not* time. Until Rob is old enough to be on his own, until he's past the age where what I do might color his thinking and feelings dramatically, it's not time. *I* might be willing to take the sort of risks that are involved in sleeping with someone outside of marriage. But they're *my* risks, and it will be *my* pain if the thing doesn't work out. I'm not willing to expose Rob to any of it.'' Caroline stopped, her chest heaving, her eyes glistening with unshed tears.

Greg stood absolutely still, watching her try to bring herself under control. He knew that he'd never been more shaken in his entire life than he was at that moment. When he'd learned his wife was going to die, he'd been utterly helpless with rage and grief, but he'd had no control over her fate or her pain. Here, he was learning that he had tremendous power to hurt this woman standing before him, and the knowledge made him quake. What if she made love with him? What if she fell in love with him and he didn't love her? Could she survive another failure? It wasn't even a matter of her surviving, really. Did he want to ask her to take the risk? She'd said Rob was more vulnerable than she was—but he didn't believe it for a moment. Could he live with himself if he hurt her?

All the while those thoughts were going through his mind, another part of him was saying, *You fool. Look at her. She's everything you'll ever want or need. Admit to yourself and to her right now that you do love her. Tell her you're willing to take the risk that she might not love you, too.*

But then another voice whispered, *She'll never believe you if you say you're in love with her. Not now.* Love and sex went together, she'd said; if he told her he loved her, she'd think he was saying it to get her to go to bed with him. As unsure as he felt at that moment, maybe that was even true. Not that he would try to trick her into bed but that, perhaps, he didn't know if what he felt for her was the lasting sort of love she needed and deserved. Could it be that all of his feelings were based on this incredible desire to touch her and to be touched by her?

In the end the fear of hurting her made him uncertain.

Caroline stood for a long time watching Greg and trying to divine his thoughts. So many emotions passed across his face as he stared at her. Finally when she couldn't stand the tension anymore, she whirled away from him and faced the row of doors, her arms wrapped around her middle, as she had stood when this whole conversation had begun. Nothing had changed, except that now she felt raw and exposed and more miserable than ever.

Taking a couple of steps toward her, Greg put a hand on her shoulder and spoke quietly. "The last thing on earth I want to do is hurt you. But I don't want you to give up on the possibility that maybe, just maybe, there's something between us worth sharing. Worth going after in spite of whatever the other priorities in our lives might be. It's so strong, Caroline! I can't believe it's not—"

He cut himself short. How could he say that he couldn't believe it wasn't love? No, she had to take that risk herself. He couldn't take it for her, and he couldn't force her into it.

"We've both got a lot to consider," he finished. "I think I'll go for a walk." When she didn't respond, he asked, "Would you like to come?"

She shook her head, then, with a sigh, turned and looked up at him. Whatever the outcome, she couldn't deny the feelings of friendship and goodwill that had been built between them. There was something about Greg that made her believe that, somehow, things would be all right. And it was that sense of sanity and reason she felt around him that allowed her to give him a shaky smile and say, "Besides, one of us has to stay with Jeb Stuart. Suppose he wakes up and cries?"

Shaking his head very slowly, Greg returned her smile with a gentle one of his own. "You're pretty amazing, do you know that?" he said. His finger touched the end of her nose in an affectionate gesture that helped ease the strain between them. "Should I offer to wash and wax your car if you stay with Jeb while I'm out?"

"That's all right," she said graciously. "Just don't be too long."

When he'd gone, Caroline took herself to the bedroom and had a good, long cry. She was beginning to wonder if any pain she might experience in loving and losing Greg could be as bad as the pain she felt in not taking the risk of loving him at all.

It was a question she carried home with her Sunday afternoon and one that continued to haunt her as the days passed.

Six

Fertilization was on the agenda for the week. And with the past weekend still fresh in Caroline's mind, the prospect of discussing any aspect of human sexuality was just short of agonizing. It seemed inevitable that everything would choose that particular time to go wrong. Film projectors broke, slides got lost and someone kept setting off the fire alarm so that most of Tuesday and Wednesday was spent outdoors. On top of all this three student egg teams broke their eggs. To these six grief-stricken "parents," Caroline could only offer a philosophic shrug as she entered their grade in her book.

One student left his egg in New York City over the weekend and spent two days trying to convince Caroline that *lost* wasn't the same as *broken*. His partner wanted to file a missing persons report with the police to try to get it back. Caroline had a good laugh over lunch on Thursday with

Sally Stimpson, as they tried to imagine what sort of description the student would give of her beloved egg child.

"Can't you see it?" Sally held out a hand as though envisioning the headlines. "Missing: three-month-old egg of unknown gender. Blue eyes, heavily rouged in aqua Day-Glo. Identifying marks include star-shaped dimples and decal with the number two thousand and one. Last seen wearing an aluminum foil helmet over white cotton ball hair and traveling in a white cylindrical container. Answers to the name 'Galaxy.' "

Caroline laughed as she put her coffee cup in its saucer. "I'm sure the New York City police would love it, though I suppose they've seen crazier things."

"Yeah, like the cafeteria yesterday afternoon. Talk about riots! Who'd have thought one little broken egg could stink up a room that size so quickly?"

"It was pretty awful," Caroline had to agree.

"I can't wait to read our first progress reports from the egg grandparents this weekend," Sally chuckled. "Have you written yours yet?"

"I'm going to do it tonight," Caroline replied, pulling off a section of the grapefruit she was eating and offering it to Sally.

"No thanks," Sally shook her head and then asked, "Off the record, how *are* things going with Rob? Are he and Kim driving you crazy with Jeb Stuart?"

"Not at all," Caroline answered easily. "Jeb lives at Kim's house in the evenings, so I never have to deal with him. Greg Lawton and his housekeeper get the honors."

"Speaking of Mr. Gregory Lawton," Sally picked up Caroline's lead, "I hear from Kim that all of you spent last weekend at the beach. Anything serious?"

Deliberately misunderstanding, Caroline answered, "Oh, I don't think so. Kim and Rob seem to have a good time with each other, but I haven't noticed any real danger signals."

"Don't be dense, Caroline," Sally admonished. "I meant between you and Mr. Lawton, and you know it. He's quite an attractive man, isn't he?"

"Mmm, I suppose so," Caroline evaded. "He's . . . very nice. And he's a great father."

"Has it crossed your mind to wonder what other fine qualities he might possess?"

Caroline started to deny any interest in Greg whatsoever, but knowing that Sally would soon worm the truth out of her anyway, she gave up. "I've thought about it," she said quietly. "I've thought about it a lot."

Sally perked up, obviously waiting for Caroline to say more. When she didn't, Sally urged her on. "Well? Has he shown an interest in *your* attributes—other than your being a fine teacher and mother?"

"Yes," Caroline sighed.

"So, how come you're looking like the dog just died?" the older woman wanted to know. "Most women would be delighted to have a gorgeous, unattached male attracted to them."

"Most women don't teach sex ed in this school district. And most women aren't single parents of an impressionable sixteen-year-old."

"An amazing number of them are."

Caroline shrugged. "How they lead their lives is their business."

"Caroline, I don't believe you," Sally groaned. "When are you going to let up on yourself? You're thirty-five, an attractive woman, and you have a right to your own life. It's unlikely that after all this time you're going to become so promiscuous that anyone would be offended."

"I'm not really worried about offending anyone," Caroline admitted, lowering her gaze. "I'm not even sure anymore if I'm really worried about Rob."

"So, what *are* you worried about?"

Toying with a corner of her napkin, Caroline answered in a tiny voice. "Well, there's me. It's always been easy to pass up opportunities for a 'sex only' relationship. But I've waited a long time for a relationship where love comes *before* sex and commitment is part of the deal. Maybe I'm being foolish and hopelessly old-fashioned, but I don't want to settle for less. I guess I'm just plain scared of getting hurt."

Sally's eyes widened a little. "Do you love Greg Lawton?"

Caroline drew a great and painful breath. "Lord, Sally, I'm afraid I do."

"Do you think he loves you?"

"Maybe. I don't know."

"But he might," Sally insisted.

"Yes," Caroline shook her head, flustered. "I guess so. Or maybe he could eventually. I don't *know*!"

"So, what's the problem?" Sally spread her hands palms up. "You date a little. You talk about it. It's called courtship, Caroline. Been going on for years."

"Yeah," Caroline rolled her eyes. "Except that every time we see each other, all either of us thinks about is..."

"Sex."

"Right."

"I see. Well, maybe you should give it a try."

"Just like that?"

Sally shrugged. "If you can't think of anything else, there must be *something* to it. Maybe it'll turn out to be the thing you've been waiting for all your life. Then again, maybe it'll be awful, and you'll wonder what you ever saw in him."

"And maybe I'll win the lottery next week and move to the Mediterranean."

"Not likely, huh?" Sally chuckled. "Well, you won't know unless you try it. And wouldn't it be better to know that you weren't missing anything than to wonder the rest of your life what you'd passed up?"

Caroline's reply was almost a whisper. "I've got a pretty good idea what I'm passing up. And it's making me crazy. I'm afraid of getting hurt. I'm afraid that Rob will suffer if I turn into an emotional wreck. Worst of all, I think I'm afraid I won't ever have a chance like this again."

"Talk about being caught between a rock and a hard place." Sally shook her head slowly, eyeing Caroline with concern. "But, Caroline, you aren't a green, wide-eyed kid anymore. What we teach our students all day—what you teach Rob—is fine for teenagers who have no experience in life. You aren't going to make the same mistakes they will. If you think there's a chance you and Greg Lawton could have something really special, I say go for it."

"That's what Greg said, more or less."

"He's really after you, huh?"

"To put it mildly."

"No wonder you're starting to look as frazzled as half the girls in this school. Does she or doesn't she? Will she or won't she? It's the same game whether you're sixteen or sixty, I guess. Makes you paranoid as the dickens."

"I'm okay," Caroline tried to shrug off her less-than-spunky appearance.

"You could be better if you quit waging war against the forces of nature and, as one old song I remember put it, 'let the sunshine in.'"

Caroline looked at her, then lowered her eyes once more. "Maybe."

* * *

The sun wasn't anywhere to be seen that night at eleven-twenty as Caroline gazed out the window for at least the seventh time in the past hour. Rob and Kim had gone to Kevin Foster's house for a committee meeting to plan the junior ring dance. It was a school night; Kim had to be home at ten, and Rob should have been home shortly thereafter.

Caroline told herself repeatedly that she wasn't worried, that Rob was probably visiting with Kim at her house. Maybe he and Greg had gotten into a conversation and Rob had forgotten the time.

Except that Rob never forgot the time. And if he was late, he called. She couldn't remember an occasion when he hadn't. She tried hard to remember one until eleven-thirty; and then she picked up the phone.

Her fingers hesitated over the buttons. It would make sense to call Greg first to see if the kids were there, but she decided against it, not wanting to face the feelings her conversation with Sally had stirred up. But when she called the Foster home and discovered that Kim and Rob had left at nine-fifteen, she didn't hesitate to punch out Greg's number.

"They aren't here, Caroline."

Greg's voice reflected concern, but to Caroline's nearly panicked way of thinking, he sounded ridiculously calm.

"But Greg, where are they?" she cried, her voice cracking despite her effort to control it.

"Take it easy, honey. They probably had car trouble or stopped to get pizza and forgot the time."

"Rob never forgets the time! *Never!* Oh, where are they, Greg?"

There was a moment of silence. Then Greg said, "Look, Mrs. Reid is here in case they come here or call. I'm coming over there to be with you."

"Greg, no," Caroline flustered. "You don't need to—"

"I'll see you in a few minutes."

He hung up. Caroline pulled on her bathrobe over her nightgown and started pacing.

When Greg arrived she was a bundle of nerves.

"I'm going to call the police and see if any accidents have been reported," she declared, walking toward the kitchen. But when she reached for the phone, Greg put his hand out to stop her.

"Caroline, it's not midnight yet," he said gently. "I know they're late, and I'm as worried as you are. But let's call the other kids who went to the meeting first. If none of them know where Rob and Kim are, then we'll call the police."

His voice was so sane. Only the tiny lines around the corners of his mouth and the fact that he kept rubbing his hand over his jaw indicated his concern. Caroline looked at Greg and suddenly realized how overwrought she really was.

"You're right," she said, making a concerted effort to match her tone to the reasonable quality in his. "I'll get the phone numbers."

Half an hour later they'd gone through the list and hadn't found anyone who knew where Kim or Rob could be. Greg was starting to actually look as worried as Caroline felt, though neither of them gave voice to any of the horrific pictures their minds were conjuring. He was picking up the phone to call the police and she was rummaging through a kitchen cabinet looking for the Alka Seltzer when they heard the front door open.

Caroline knocked a bottle of Worcestershire sauce onto the floor, and Greg slammed the phone back on the hook. Both of them dashed toward the front hall.

"Hi, Mom. Mr. Lawton." Rob met them at the bottom of the stairs. He glanced warily at Greg then back at Caroline. "Golly, Mom, I'm sorry. I guess you two have been worried."

With an effort Caroline restrained herself from bursting into tears of relief. Her voice was shaky but controlled as she asked, "Rob, where have you been?"

"Is Kim at home?" Greg put in quickly.

Rob nodded. "Yes, sir. I dropped her off about ten minutes ago. Neither of you is going to believe this, but I swear, it's the truth. We've been looking for Jeb Stuart."

Caroline sucked in her breath, and she heard Greg make some inarticulate noise deep in his throat; both of them, by unspoken agreement, waited for Rob to finish his explanation.

"We left Kevin's house a little after nine," Rob went on, "and stopped at Listrani's for a pizza and Coke. Just as we got there, the movie next door let out, and the place got real crowded. I went over to the counter to order, and while I was gone, Kim had to use the ladies' room. She left Jeb Stuart on our table, figuring he was safer there than in a packed rest room. When she got back he was gone, box and all. We've spent the last two and a half hours looking for him."

"Rob, why didn't you call me?" Caroline asked, unable to keep a quaver out of her voice.

"Mom." He shook his head slowly. "I didn't even think about it. Can you believe it? Kim was running all over the place, crying like crazy and acting sort of hysterical. And I was... well, I was pretty worried myself." He shrugged a little, trying to be nonchalant. "I mean, I don't want to flunk, you know."

"Did you find the egg?" Greg asked, managing an almost casual tone.

"Yeah!" Rob perked up instantly. "We looked everywhere! Finally we figured out that the girl who was cleaning tables took him, thinking the last people at the table left him. But by then she'd gone home for the night, and we still had to find him. He wasn't in any of the garbage cans.'' Rob shuddered a little, visibly, and let out a long breath. "I think Kim would have really flipped out if we'd found Jeb Stuart in a trash compactor. Finally we found him in the manager's office. I guess the girl must have thought whoever left him would come back. Then we had to explain to everybody who'd helped us look what this crazy box with the egg in it was. That took forever! We were at your house, Mr. Lawton, when we cooled out enough to realize you two were probably getting worried. Mrs. Reid said you'd come over here, so I figured I might as well come on home rather than take the time to call. Another ten minutes didn't seem like it was going to matter much.''

"It might have made the difference between the police being called or not,'' Greg told him soberly.

Rob's eyes widened. "Really? You were that worried? Gosh, I'm sorry. Mom, you know I'd never—''

"It's all right, Rob,'' Caroline cut in. "I understand. I'm not going to yell at you for not calling once in sixteen years. But Greg's right. Next time phone as soon as you remember. Please.''

He nodded. "If it's okay with you, I think I'll go to bed. This egg parent business really takes it out of you. You know what I mean?''

Caroline felt rather than saw Greg smile along with her. "Yes, Rob, I know exactly what you mean,'' she said.

Rob trudged on to bed, and Caroline and Greg watched him go. Then, with a sigh, Caroline turned and walked into the living room to stand in front of the sofa. She stared at the watercolor on the wall over the small electric fireplace. It was a painting Rob had done of their Christmas tree when he was seven years old. There were two presents under the brightly decorated spruce; a card on one of them read, *To Rob with love, Mom*. The other package declared, *I love you, Mom. From Rob*.

Coming up behind her, Greg said softly, "Did it occur to you that if you put your mind to it, you and your egg experiment could single-handedly wipe out the entire human race? Rob didn't exactly look like he was ready for the joys of parenthood, did he?"

With her eyes still fixed on Rob's telling representation of their family life, Caroline gave a short laugh. With a trace of bitterness she replied, "Oh, I rather imagine, that with the right person, the urge to procreate would always be irresistible. Rob will end up feeling like the rest of us jaded, old folk that the rewards far outweigh the...the risks. Oh, Greg, I was so *scared*."

Caroline's hands covered her face. Her insides felt as though they were made of jelly, and a bubble of hysteria seemed to swell inside of her, looking for a chance to break. The chance came when Greg reached out and pulled her against him.

"It's all right, honey," he told her softly, smoothing back her hair and placing a kiss on her forehead. "Everything's all right now."

His tenderness, his very presence, undid her completely; before she could stop herself, she began to cry. When she realized what she was doing, her first reaction was to cover her mouth and glance toward the stairs.

Greg instantly understood her concern that Rob might hear and looked for a solution to the problem. When he saw a door leading to what he guessed would be a den, he pulled Caroline through it. Once inside, he switched on a lamp and glanced briefly around the tiny room. It contained only a small desk and an armchair. Still holding Caroline's hand, he closed the door behind them.

"All right, honey," he told her, pulling her back into his arms. "Now you can cry your eyes out."

Caroline, who had been choking back each sob that shuddered through her, didn't need any further encouragement. "Oh, Greg!" she burst out. "What if they hadn't been all right? What if they'd had an accident? I don't know if I could stand it if Rob were killed! I think I'd die! It hurts just *thinking* about it!"

"Don't," he ordered, his arms tightening their hold. "You'll go crazy thinking about all the things that can happen to a child once you've had him."

"I know!" she cried, her voice muffled against his chest. "I've tried for years not to think about all those things, but I can't help it! Sometimes it gets to me, how terrifying a job being a parent really is. And I think to myself, what are you *doing*, Caroline? What are you doing with all this responsibility? Why don't you give it to someone else and . . . and run away to *Fiji* or some place else they'll never find you? But there isn't anyone to give it to! There's only me! That's all there's *ever* been! And oh, dear God, I'm so tired of it being this way!"

Greg squeezed his eyes closed. Did it ever get any easier? Why did it have to hurt so much, watching someone you loved suffer pain? From the bottom of his soul he wanted to tell Caroline that she never had to be alone again. That he loved her and wanted to be with her, not only to share the trials of parenting but to share every aspect of their lives. He wanted to take the risk of loving with her—for better or worse, until death, as he knew it always would, did eventually part them.

Knowing he couldn't push her into something she didn't want, too, the most he could say was, "Caroline, you're not alone right now."

She pulled back to look at him, tears streaming down her face as her eyes searched his. Suddenly her breath caught, and her tears stopped flowing.

"You are here, aren't you?" she breathed in wonder—and a moment later, a horrified look came over her face. "I must be out of my mind! Greg, what am I doing to myself? What am I doing to *you*? Why am I keeping us from having something else, something *good* to think about when things get hard? Why am I making us both be alone when neither of us really wants to be alone at all? And why on earth won't I give us the chance to share our lives—our*selves*—with each other the way we both know we want to?"

"Caroline..." Greg's heart slammed against the wall of his chest, his whole body growing rigid with tension. "Caroline, are you saying you want to make love with me?"

Caroline's eyes were locked with his. *Yes*, that was what she was saying, and it seemed exactly right. What she felt wasn't adolescent fancy for a boy she barely knew but deep, lasting love for a man who would never hurt her.

"Yes," she whispered. "Greg, I want to make love with you."

"Oh, honey, are you sure?" His voice was hoarse, and his fingers trembled as they came up to touch her tear-moistened cheek. "Are you sure you aren't reacting to being scared? Maybe we should wait—"

"Please," she cut him off. "I want you so badly. I don't care anymore what anyone else thinks. I don't care whether I'm reacting to the moment. I want to make love with you. Now."

With a muttered curse that sounded oddly like an endearment, Greg locked the door and enveloped her in a kiss that held no restraint. He didn't care, either, what anyone thought or whether this was an act of momentary weakness on her part. He didn't care about anything but the fact that

she was here in his arms, asking him to fulfill his most treasured fantasy. And he complied with her request with a fury
and passion that consumed them both.

His mouth moved feverishly across her face, her throat,
behind her ear as he muttered, "Caroline. Oh, Carrie, it's
going to be so good!"

"Yes!" she gasped, crying and laughing in pure relief as
the boundaries of her circumscribed life fell away and a
world full of pleasure and tenderness and passion opened up
before her. The boundaries of the new world were described by the circle of Greg's arms as they held her, and at
that moment it seemed those arms provided all the space she
would ever need. She reveled in the textures and tastes of his
mouth as it joined hers once more. Her fingers sought to
learn every contour of muscle and bone as they ran across
his shoulders and down his arms over and over again.

With a deep groan Greg slid his hand inside the neck of
her robe and pushed it off one slender shoulder. His mouth
followed the trail his fingers had left, and the gap in the
front of the robe widened. Soon she was bent over his arm,
and he was kissing the skin exposed between her breasts.
Her hands clung to his upper arms as she panted his name.
She didn't notice when he untied her robe or when the straps
of her nightgown fell down her arms. But the devouring heat
of his mouth covering her breast made her cry out, and she
arched sharply against him, her fingers digging into his
flesh.

She was beautiful, he told her; she was sweet and soft and
warm, and so many other things that made Caroline tremble with longing to hear him say them. He lavished her with
praise the whole time he was tasting and nibbling and sucking the silky-smooth flesh of her breasts. Then he moved
upward to bury his face against her neck, declaring,

"Caroline, you make me want so much! I've *never* wanted like this! Never!"

Nor had she. But she had neither the words nor the chance to tell him. Not once did he pause to let either of them catch their breath in his relentless assault on her senses. It could have been frightening, how out of control his passion was, but he didn't give her time to be afraid. With his mouth and his hands on her body he drove them both from the edges of desire into its core.

Hungrily, he feasted upon her breasts once more, until the tingling, aching feeling that radiated from the hardened peaks was nearly unbearable. Then she felt searing kisses move across her ribs and belly as he dropped to his knees. His lips touched a bare thigh, and the heat washed through her, melting her to the bone. His arms went around her hips and he caressed the smooth, sensual curve of her belly with his cheek. His mouth nudged the hidden warmth between her thighs.

"Greg!" Her hands moved through his hair as she held his head to her. "Oh, Greg, you make me weak!"

"And you make me crazy," he growled, urging her down to kneel in the cradle of his slightly spread thighs. Even then he didn't stop but pulled her into the frame of his hard body for yet another shattering kiss. From thighs to breasts, Caroline felt the heat of him burning into her through the barrier of his clothing until, finally, she drew back, gulping air and staring at him, mesmerized.

"Your mouth," she breathed, fascinated by that part of him which had beguiled her with its secrets of arousal. Her fingertips grazed across his lips.

He caught them with his teeth and sucked them inside. His eyes locked with hers in a moment of erotic pleasure that made Caroline think the rest of the world must surely have drifted far, far away. The real world existed solely in the moist heat of his mouth, the elusive smoky color of his eyes, the sound of their ragged breathing. Slowly, she pulled her fingers from him and placed her lips over his; their mouths were fused and their breathing became one.

Without breaking the kiss, Greg lowered Caroline until she was stretched out beneath him on the carpet. Kneeling above her, his eyes locked with hers, he tore his shirt over his head. His belt was ripped open, and his slacks and briefs were kicked away. For a long, long moment they looked at one another. Just looked. And wanted.

Then, still kneeling, he straddled her hips, and his hands began moving over her, lightly at first—a finger trailing over her thigh, a palm lightly molding her breast. He took his time at first, but, as their mutual need drove them on, his exploration picked up pace. His mouth joined his hands, and then it was as if he were trying to touch all of her at once. Caroline was already wild with need when his fingers parted the damp folds of heated flesh hidden between her thighs. There his hand stayed...and stayed...and stayed yet a little longer to touch and excite her beyond any point of reason.

With her own hands, she stroked and encouraged and tried to tell him of her need. Finally her fingers came together to surround his masculinity. He choked out her name and fell forward, her hands still between them, lowering his body onto hers, rubbing his hardness into the softness of her belly.

Caroline sobbed, begging him to fulfill the promise his body was making to hers. "Oh, Greg, please. I can't stand it! Just looking at you makes me come apart. What you're doing! I feel like...like..."

"Like you're going to explode," he finished roughly. "You are, Caroline. With me inside you."

Shivering, she gave a long, throaty moan and buried her face against his neck. The musky scent of him, the harsh sound of his breathing—he was the focus of all her senses. He shifted a little, and she felt the intimate probing of his hard male flesh. Her heart raced, and every muscle in her body tensed as her hips arched to meet him.

"Easy, honey," he whispered against her ear. "I don't want to hurt you."

The thought that he might never entered her head, though perhaps it should have. It had been a very long time. But she was mindless with the need to have him inside her, and his barely audible whisper of caution did nothing to quell that need. Then, as she started to tell him to please, please hurry, he entered her with a single, gliding thrust. Her breath caught, and her eyes squeezed closed.

"Caroline?"

Her breath rushed out in a moan of the deepest pleasure she'd ever felt. "Ohhh, *Greg*!"

He filled her perfectly, full and deep. It was all so new. So vastly different. So wonderfully and completely right. She'd never dreamed anything like it existed. It could have been the first time for her, and in many ways it was. Tenderness. Passion. Strength and pure sensual abandonment. Gentleness. And a nearly violent desire that took her breath away. She found all these things and more—so much more—in the way he loved her. When the end came, their gazes were locked. Tears of unimagined pleasure streamed down Caroline's face as the waves of fulfillment rocked through her. But the joy came in watching the look of glory and awe and unbridled possession that transformed Greg's countenance as his body poured itself into hers.

"Caroline?"

"Hmmm?"

"Are you going to regret this?"

"No."

"You sure? I haven't made love on the floor in...well, in a long time. I'm afraid it's an indication of the state of mind you put me in that I didn't even ask if you wanted to go upstairs."

She smiled. "You think you could have made it up the steps?"

Greg thought about it for a moment. "I'm not sure. How about you?"

"Am I here with you or not?"

He pushed up to lean on one forearm and gaze down at her. "Yeah, you're here. And, oh, you are beautiful."

Caroline's eyes sparkled as they coasted over him, then coming back to meet his gaze, she spoke gently. "I'm rather impressed myself."

He grinned. "That's good. At forty-two a man is starting to reach the age where he needs to hear that sort of thing once in a while."

"Being thirty-five doesn't exactly inspire self-confidence in a woman, either," she returned, lowering her gaze. "But you make me feel beautiful."

"Caroline?"

"Hmm?"

"I think I'm going to make you feel beautiful again. Very soon."

"Rob will sleep like the living dead if I don't take off his Walkman earphones. And I don't think one night will destroy his hearing forever, do you?"

"Uh-uh." His fingers traced an imaginary line up her arm, over her shoulder and downward to the rosy tip of one breast. "I've got a flight out at noon. That means being at the airport by eleven at the latest. I should go home."

"Oh, well, I suppose you should."

Seven

At five a.m., Greg dragged himself out of Caroline's bed, saying that, unless she were willing to explain to his co-captain why he was napping in the cockpit, he'd better go home so he could get some real sleep. Hating to see him go but knowing he had to leave before Rob woke up, Caroline pulled on her robe and followed him down the stairs.

At the front door she threw back the dead bolt and opened the door a few inches. Then she stopped and looked up at Greg with a smile that was soft and sleepy. He put his hands on her shoulders and pulled her to him, nuzzling his cheek against the silkiness of her hair.

"My return flight gets in tomorrow at three o'clock. Will you have dinner with me?"

Caroline nodded, her fingers idling over his shirt front. Yes, she'd have dinner with him and whatever else might follow. At that moment she would have said yes to any-thing he'd asked of her.

"Damn, I hate leaving you," he muttered, bending to place a kiss behind her right ear.

She turned to meet his lips on their way to hers, and they both made little sounds of satisfaction.

Caroline pulled away before things became too heated. "Go sleep," she told him. "It's all right if I'm worthless today. All I have to do is watch a movie about prenatal nutrition, which I've already seen. It's *not* okay if you're exhausted thirty thousand feet off the ground."

"How early can I pick you up tomorrow night?"

She thought a minute. "Rob has a lawn to cut after school, and I like to have dinner waiting for him. Make it seven."

"Okay," he agreed, then kissed her again. This time, it was Greg who pulled back, saying, "You make me feel like a kid, Caroline Forrester. I can't get enough of you."

Caroline actually giggled, an unheard-of event in her up-until-now sober existence. But then she felt very young herself as she answered, "Your appetite seems about right to me, Gregory Lawton. Now get out of here, will you, or I'll spend the day worrying about whether you'll fly your plane into the Golden Gate Bridge!"

He chuckled and gave her a quick kiss on the forehead before she shoved him out the door. Caroline leaned against the door frame and watched as he got into his car and drove off. With a sigh that was tired and relaxed and very happy, she closed the door and turned.

And then her heart took one gigantic leap to her throat, and her stomach knotted violently.

"Rob! What are you—" she choked off, an instant rush of heat scorching her from head to toes.

Rob stood halfway down the stairs, staring at her. He was dressed in his shorts and a T-shirt, and his earphones were dangling around his neck. "I got up to go to the bathroom and I heard the door open,'' he explained in a voice that told Caroline nothing about his feelings. "I thought I ought to check it out.''

Caroline was utterly speechless. She tried to think of something reasonable to say, some explanation to offer as to why Greg Lawton was leaving their house at five in the morning. But what *could* she say? The truth was obvious. Anything else would sound absurd.

Rob solved the problem for her. "Guess I'll go back to bed,'' he mumbled, then turned and walked up the stairs.

Caroline waited until she heard his door close, then crept quietly up to her own room. Falling onto her back on the bed, her hands came up to cover her face, and she groaned aloud.

What had she *done*?

Her eyes opened, and she took in the sight of her bed. The rose-colored spread was on the floor at the foot of it, and the top sheet was draped over the spread in a twisted lump. Pillows were scattered everywhere. Looking around, she noticed her nightgown on the floor by the closed door. There were half-empty glasses of iced tea on the night table. Two of them. And the room was filled with the scents of lovemaking. Heady, erotic scents of heated flesh and fulfillment.

What she'd done was to have the most incredibly lovely, pleasure-filled night of her entire life. As she put the room in order and showered, she found herself blushing at the memories of that loveliness and pleasure. She still felt flutters of arousal whenever she pictured some particularly intimate moment with Greg. Even the shock of having Rob discover what had taken place couldn't completely dispel the mellow, floating feeling of satisfaction.

It did, however, taint that satisfaction with a hint of shame—which was something she knew she had no business feeling. People had made her ashamed of her sexuality once before, and she had vowed never to let it happen again. She still had vivid memories of her father standing over her, yelling that she was a cheap slut and certainly no daughter of his. She could hear herself crying, "But, Daddy, where will I go?" And she could hear Chuck whining, "Jeez, Caroline, I guess we better get married but it sure isn't what I'd planned." It wasn't what she had planned, either.

Caroline was fully aware that lovemaking with Greg had nothing in common with the fumbling and, for her, painful scene that had taken place in Chuck's Chevy all those years ago. She'd told Greg she wasn't going to regret making love with him. And she wasn't. She couldn't. But that didn't make it right. A person could make a mistake they didn't regret. And that it had been a mistake was, to her, a foregone conclusion.

After all these years of protecting Rob from the embarrassment of having a father *and* a mother who failed to exercise judgment in their moral behavior, she'd blown it in one impulsive moment. The only thing to do, she knew, was to be truthful with Rob; she would tell him that, yes, she and Greg were attracted to one another and, yes, they'd both succumbed to their attraction but that it wouldn't happen again. She could explain that sometimes a person did things which they didn't regret, exactly, but which they came to realize were the wrong thing at the wrong time. In other words, a person was not obligated to repeat his or her mistakes. Yes, that sounded about right for Rob.

But what on earth was she going to tell Greg?

That question plagued her as she got dressed and fixed breakfast for her son. She couldn't have eaten a bite herself. When Rob came ambling down the stairs at seven dressed for school, she wasn't ready to face him and so scurried off, ostensibly to get ready to leave. At seven-fifteen when they got in the car, Caroline prepared herself for one of the hardest conversations of her life.

She waited until Rob had pulled the car out of their parking lot and onto the road. Then, determinedly, she began, "Rob, about this morning."

"You don't have to explain anything, Mom," he said, his eyes focused straight ahead on the road.

"No, I owe you an explanation," Caroline persisted doggedly.

"Kim and I already figured out that you and Mr. Lawton were, well, that you liked each other."

That shocked her. In a quick sideways glance, Caroline looked at her son. "You did?"

He shrugged. "Sure. I could see the night we all went roller-skating that he had a case for you. And since then, he's always asking me how you are and stuff. Then there was that night after the rock concert. You two had been...that is, Kim and I got back at a bad time, didn't we?"

Caroline stammered a little, and Rob cut her off.

"It's okay, Mom. It isn't any of my business. Then at the beach last weekend it was pretty obvious you were both uptight about something. The way you kept looking at each other was awesome. So, this morning, well..." He shrugged again as though to say he'd rather expected the whole thing.

Rob's reaction, and his and Kim's assumptions, did nothing at all to relieve Caroline's mind. In fact it appalled her that her son and his girlfriend had been discussing their parents like they might have discussed a couple of their teenage friends. Wasn't this exactly the sort of thing she'd been working to avoid? A child, and an adolescent especially, had enough problems; growing up was hard work, and a parent's job was to make the process easier, not more difficult. Boys on the verge of adulthood were supposed to be especially sensitive about their mothers as sexual beings—

at least that's what all the books said. And in any case it wasn't fair to expect a sixteen-year-old to cope with the ups and downs of his parent's love life.

"I'm sorry, Rob," she said, speaking the first words that came to her mind. "I'm sorry you and Kim have been worried. And I'm sorry to have embarrassed you this morning."

"Mom, stop it, will you?" Rob exclaimed. "It's no big deal. Really."

"But I don't want you to think—"

"The only thing I think is that Mr. Lawton's a great guy and that you wouldn't go getting yourself into something you couldn't handle. Okay?"

Caroline's lips thinned. She simply couldn't accept that Rob was taking the news that his mother was having an affair so casually. It didn't seem, well, *normal*! It also didn't seem like Rob; he was usually very interested in her social behavior due, perhaps, to the lingering insecurity from his father's cavalier treatment.

Cautiously Caroline asked, "Aren't you afraid this is going to mess things up for you and Kim? I mean, suppose Greg and I were to part company on a sour note."

"Kim and I already decided we'd cool it as far as dating goes," Rob told her with remarkable calm.

Caroline gave him a wide-eyed stare. Last weekend she'd seen him kissing Kim, and things had looked anything but cool. "When did this happen?" she asked, disbelieving.

"Sunday on the drive home from the beach. We like each other a lot, but we aren't in love or anything. And we decided that if things ever got serious between you and Mr. Lawton—like if you ever got married, even—we wouldn't want to wind up living in the same house knowing *too much* about one another."

For the second time that morning Caroline was speechless. Was this her baby? When had he grown up? When had he learned to make decisions that reflected such sensitivity and a willingness to sacrifice his own pleasure for others? This wasn't the decision of an awkward adolescent. It was the conclusion a mature, clear thinking adult might reach. It was also a decision two single-parented children might concoct if they harbored hopes of forming a family. In either case the knowledge of what Kim and Rob had decided between them both scared and shamed her.

While the children had been planning their lives around their parents, she and Greg had been thinking only of their own desires. Oh, she'd tried to keep in mind her responsibilities, but when the crunch came, she hadn't been able to pull it off. She'd told Greg that she didn't care what anyone thought of their making love. And at that moment she hadn't. What sort of a mother exercised less control over her sexual behavior than her teenage son?

Dear heavens, she and Greg hadn't even been out on a single date together! Granted, it wasn't for Greg's lack of trying, but hadn't his desire to date her been motivated by his far more powerful desire to make love with her? When she'd presented him with the opportunity to satisfy the latter without the bother of the former, he hadn't balked. He hadn't said, "Now, Caroline, I think we should get to know each other better before we think about making love. I want you to know that I respect you. I want you to know that my attraction for you has to do with more than sex."

No, he hadn't said anything like that. *Nobody* had ever said anything like that to her. And she resented it like hell. Never in her life had she been given the chance to...to be courted. Not by a man who truly cared about her. Perhaps her own rigid standards had been partly to blame but she wasn't sure of that. Her caution didn't entirely account for the infrequency with which she dated. Her lack of social life had more to do with the sort of men who asked her out. Most of the time they were simply male friends. Other times they were men who had no interest in building a long-term relationship—men who wanted only one thing: having a good time without paying the consequences.

Some people, as she well knew, never grew up.

Caroline also knew that Greg wasn't like that. And feeling the way they did toward each other, she knew they would never be able to be simply good friends. But when it came down to it, she wondered exactly what he did feel for her. It had practically killed her not to tell him she loved him when they'd made love. It had seemed so natural. So right. And it was the truth. But it felt too soon to say it, and she was scared of being hurt. If she'd said it, would he have said it, too? And would he have meant it?

He wanted to go to dinner with her tomorrow night. Would he still want to go if he didn't think the evening would end in lovemaking? Would he understand that, at this point, *not* making love with him was really a sign of how much importance she placed on their relationship? Would he understand how much it meant to her to have him pay her that special attention a woman dreams of having from the man she loves?

Maybe it wasn't too late, after all, to experience the sort of courtship she'd missed when circumstances had forced her to grow up too soon. She was more than willing to be wooed by a marriage-minded man. It remained to be seen whether or not Greg would be willing to play the handsome beau.

"Greg, please. Don't—"

"Don't stop?"

"No. Don't *do* that."

"Don't kiss you?" Greg drew back and looked at Caroline a little startled. They were sitting in the car in front of her house, having come back from dinner. "Why don't you want me to kiss you, honey?"

Her brows drew together in a tiny frown, and she looked at her hands folded over the purse in her lap. "I just don't."

Confused, he asked, "Are you worried about somebody seeing us out here?"

She shrugged a little. "That and, well, other things."

"What other things?"

She was quiet for a moment. Then, in a rush, came, "I have something I need to say. I don't want us to make love again."

Greg blinked, wondering which of a hundred questions to ask first, but before he could ask any of them, she went on. And his heart sunk.

"Rob saw you leave yesterday morning. It was, well, awkward. As you can imagine."

"And now you're ashamed of what we did and want to take it back," he concluded instantly.

"No," she shook her head. "I'm not ashamed of making love with you. I'm simply determined not to *become* ashamed of what I've done to my son."

"We've been through this before," Greg cut in, his patience wearing a little thin. "You've told me that you wanted Rob to grow up thinking that sex is special and that he should consider the consequences of his actions. I agree with you entirely. But, for God's sake, Caroline! You're expecting an awful lot of *me*, if you think I can pretend that what we shared the other night never happened! Don't you realize how important it was to me?"

There was a long moment of silence. Finally Greg sighed in frustration and flopped back against his seat to stare out the window. His bent elbow rested on the open window, and his fingers drummed rhythmically against the roof of the car.

A moment later Caroline spoke quietly. "Are you saying you don't want to see me again if we can't make love?"

Greg's fingers stopped drumming, and he turned his head to study her closely. He was angry. And hurt. He'd flown six thousand miles since he'd left her the morning before, and every one of them had been spent thinking about her. Thinking about how much he loved her. How could she believe he didn't want to see her again? How could she even *dream* it?

But wait. There was something here she wasn't saying. He could sense it in her voice, in the way her fingers were gripping her purse as though they'd crush it. She'd been nervous all evening; he'd thought it was excitement but maybe...

Was she scared? Scared of him? Scared he would say, no, he didn't want to continue their relationship without sex being a part of it? It seemed improbable given what he knew about her. If she'd been anyone else but who she was, he would have thought she was playing a very childish game: trying to get him to prove he liked her for herself and not for what she could give him. But Caroline wouldn't do that. She was a very mature woman. She'd raised a child alone and put herself through school. She'd earned the professional respect of an entire community of critical, demanding parents who expected nothing but the absolute best from their children's teachers.

And she'd never had a real love affair in her life.

That thought brought his worried musings to a dead halt. What a blind fool he was being! She wasn't telling him she didn't want to make love with him anymore. She wasn't even telling him that she was worried about what others would think. She might have used that as an excuse, but if she'd really been worried, she wouldn't have made love with him at all. Caroline was a very determined woman, and no amount of sexual attraction could have made her risk a career and a child's respect that cheaply. What she was saying was that she'd become a wife at seventeen and a mother at eighteen without ever having been out on a single date. The only affair she'd had since had been with a man with whom she'd discovered she had nothing in common. Was it really so childish for a woman who'd survived those experiences to want proof of a man's interest in her beyond sex?

No. In fact the more he considered the question, the more hopeful he became. It wasn't the sort of thing she could ask for directly—having to ask made the gift worthless. But unless he was badly mistaken, she was telling him in the only way she could that she wanted him to give her what she'd missed—in short, to court her. And if that were true, she must be thinking in long-range terms. Was she falling in love with him? Lord, he hoped so.

He'd had a lot of practice being faithful to a woman who, for the better part of six years, was too ill to have an intimate relationship. Caroline wasn't ill, and it would be torture now that he knew what he was missing. But if giving her the romance she needed was what it took, he was more than willing to oblige. Hell, he could do with a little romance himself. After all, it had been a very long time for him, too.

"Caroline," he began with infinite tenderness, "I'd want to go on seeing you no matter what rules you set down. Making love with you was one of the most wonderful things that's ever happened to me, but if you can't continue that intimacy with a clear conscience, there's no point in doing it. We'd both end up being miserable."

She peeked at him hesitantly. "You're not angry?"

He shook his head. "I can't deny I'm disappointed, but I'm a grown man, not a boy. I'll survive. And meanwhile it will give us a chance to do other things together. That is, if you want to.''

Caroline's nervousness and fear evaporated in a cloud of happiness. "Oh, yes," she said, in a voice that was more breath than sound. Then her gaze lowered again as she added, "I'm afraid I always do things a little backward, Greg. I hadn't planned to start a serious relationship any time soon. It seemed like . . . bad timing, I guess. I wanted to wait until Rob was a little older. Until my job was more secure. But, well, here we are. I know I'm asking a lot of you right now, but it's very important to me."

It was as close as she could get to an admission that his reasoning had been correct, and Greg wasn't going to push her any further. Instead he said, "It's not too late to turn things around, honey. For instance—" he smiled a little, crookedly "—do you realize how little we really know about one another?"

"It is rather appalling, isn't it?" she sighed. "Under the circumstances, that is."

"Well, how about if we go back to the beginning and start over." When she looked at him curiously, he grinned. "Ya wanna hit the roller rink with me Friday night?"

At that Caroline laughed. "You mean you're willing to suffer through another night of getting your ankles kicked?"

"And another night of getting to hold your hand—and maybe a little more of you while I'm at it? Or do the rules say hands off entirely?"

Caroline blushed. "No, I think hand-holding and whatever else can go on in the middle of a hundred other people will be fine. I'd love to go."

Thus began the courtship of Caroline Forrester. And a bolder campaign for the hand of a woman had never been waged. Fresh flowers arrived at the door of her townhouse before old ones had begun to wilt. Phone calls became daily events, even when Greg was out of town. On Mother's Day Caroline suffered the good-natured teasing of her students and colleagues when Greg, not her son, sent her two dozen rainbow-colored balloons. The balloons were accompanied by a note that said she'd be getting a box of her favorite chocolates delivered once-a-month for the next year. All these things, Greg considered to be *de rigueur* in the proceedings of a normal courtship. It was the not-so-normal things he did that soon had Caroline believing she was living in a real, live fairy tale.

Since their relationship had begun at the wrong end of the courtship spectrum, Greg set out to put it back on track by covering unexplored territory. There would be no candlelit dinners in quiet, little restaurants for quite a while, he decided. Nor would they be taking any leisurely strolls down secluded country paths—even if one or two he knew had delightful "resting" places along the way. Trips to the beach cottage were out as well, in spite of the fact that May was one of the best times of year to be on the Outer Banks. In short, Greg planned dates that took the emphasis off intimacy and put it where he thought it belonged, on having fun. Fun was something of a new experience for Caroline, he knew. And, as her enjoyment became his, he began to think that this courtship business was really a pretty good idea. He also stopped wondering how long it would be before he had to make love to her again or lose his mind.

They took paddleboats out on the Tidal Basin. Greg entered them in the annual kite flying contest held in front of the Washington Monument. They went to *La Niçoise*, an expensive restaurant in Washington, where the waiters wore roller skates and entertained the guests with a variety of bawdy cabaret numbers. For a week afterward Caroline blushed every time Greg leered at her in an imitation of one of the more risqué selections they'd witnessed.

The weekend before school was out Greg rented a plane and flew her to his fraternity reunion at the University of Virginia in Charlottesville. But that extravagance was exceeded when he discovered that she loved ballet and promptly bought tickets to take her to the Kennedy Center twice a week while the American Ballet Theater was in town. Caroline was overwhelmed.

And so, it appeared, was everyone else. Kim and Rob observed their parents' activity without comment but with obvious interest. Caroline's friends, Greg's friends, and the Lawton's housekeeper did the same. It seemed that everyone loved a good romance.

To Caroline's way of thinking, the one between she and Greg was like something out of a storybook. She paid no attention to what anyone was saying or thinking. Quite simply, she didn't care. She was in love. And she was having a glorious time, learning what it meant to have a relationship with a man who, she wanted to believe, loved her as much as she loved him.

Not once during all this time did Greg so much as mention making love, though she could see in his eyes and in his smile that he thought about it. And so did she. The physical intimacy they did share only added fuel to an increasingly hot fire. They held hands. They kissed good night at her door. Greg was constantly finding reasons to touch her. And Caroline found plenty of her own to touch him. But they both seemed to sense that the next time they made love, it would be for keeps; they wanted it to be very special. And they wanted to be very sure of themselves and of each other.

It was slightly terrifying, Caroline decided, being this happy, but she chose to ignore the voice that told her she'd be smart to protect herself from the possibility that, sooner or later, she would discover that Greg wasn't really as perfect for her as he appeared to be. But that moment never came. And things got better and better.

Even Greg's schedule, which she resented at first, began to seem like a trivial matter. She had other friends, after all, a career she enjoyed, and her son. It pleased her no end to think that, soon, she might also have a step-daughter. When Greg was away, she wouldn't be flat broke, stuck at home with a new baby and wondering when—or if—her husband was coming home.

As the semester ended and summer school began, Caroline was quite sure that Greg's courtship would end with a proposal of marriage. Hesitantly at first, then with increasing daring, she began to dream of a wedding. A real wedding, with flowers and a cake and friends smiling their approval of what she and Greg were doing. It would be nothing like the wretched, hurried affair on that sweltering afternoon so many years ago. Then, the justice of the peace had been slightly drunk, and Chuck had been dressed in the same clothes he'd worn to change the oil in his car that morning. She'd had to interrupt the ceremony to go to throw up when her morning sickness had gotten the better of her, and her friend, Meg, had cried the entire time as though it were a burial service she was witnessing and not a wedding at all.

Meg had been right. It hadn't been a wedding. And what came after it could hardly be called a marriage. But as Caroline began to see what marriage to Greg could be like, she also began to envision a wedding that would do justice to the way she felt about the tender and giving man who had stolen her heart. It would be a wedding that celebrated their love—a ceremony that formalized their commitment. This wasn't a secret fantasy she'd harbored for years, a fairy tale of white knights and quests for love that had survived through the disillusionment of an ill-fated marriage and long years of loneliness. Nor was it a fantasy of hopeless longing for something she didn't ever expect to have. Rather, it was an idea springing from a seed which had lain dormant within her, waiting for the right circumstances—and the right man—to bring it to fruition.

By the time the Fourth of July had been duly celebrated on the mall in Washington with Greg and their children, Caroline couldn't imagine there being anything that would stand in the way of her dreams coming true.

But then, on the fifth of July, she remembered it was always the *un*imaginable things, happening at the worst possible moments, that had a way of turning dreams into nightmares. And as she drove into the school parking lot late that Friday morning, it seemed as though she were living one of those nightmares.

Hoping Sally would still be there, Caroline walked to the second floor and stopped short in the open doorway of her friend's classroom. Sally was seated at her desk. She looked up and smiled at Caroline, beckoning her inside. Caroline didn't smile back, and her legs, as she crossed the room, were shaky.

"Lord, Caroline," Sally greeted her with a soulful moan. "Don't call that substitute anymore. He's awful. Of course being so close to the end of the summer session didn't help. The kids this year are—" Sally broke off, suddenly registering Caroline's appearance. "Good grief, what's wrong with you?"

Having collapsed in the chair next to Sally's desk, Caroline stared at her friend, her brain a jumble of disconnected thoughts.

"Caroline?" Sally inquired hesitantly, a startled expression on her face.

Caroline tried to speak but her mouth opened and closed without a sound. Finally she had to wrap her arms around her middle and squeeze, in an effort to force the air out of her lungs. The sound came, barely audible and almost incomprehensible.

"I'm pregnant."

For an instant it seemed to Caroline that the world had come to a standstill. When the roaring pressure in her head reached the point where she thought she might explode, the words finally came tumbling out.

"But I can't be! Oh, Sally, it's not possible! It was only that one time, and he's had a vasectomy, and it *can't* be true!" Caroline's fist hit the desk beside her. Then, with a little whimper, she dropped one hand into her lap and covered her face with the other.

Sally stared at Caroline's bowed head. "Caroline? Oh, Caroline, are you really sure?"

Without raising her head, Caroline nodded vigorously.

"And you're sure about the vasectomy? He wouldn't have... No, he wouldn't have lied. But you know sometimes they fail. Very, very rarely, it's true, but it's not impossible. You said his wife died of leukemia. Maybe she was infertile from the disease and they never realized—"

"I know, I know," came the muttered interruption.

"Have you told Greg?" Sally asked.

"He's out of town until late this afternoon. I didn't know until I went to the doctor's this morning. You know how exhausted I've been this last month or so. I thought it was because of the schedule Greg and I have been keeping. And last month when I missed my period, I'd had a twenty-four hour bug and figured it was that. It never once occurred to me.... Oh God, Sally, what am I going to do?"

A perplexed frown appeared on Sally's forehead. "Well, I think the answer to that is obvious. You tell Greg. You get married. And you have a baby."

"No." The refusal was immediate and irrefutable. Caroline raised her gaze to meet Sally's stunned look. "I'm not going to have another shotgun wedding. I'm not going to live through another marriage where my husband feels he's been trapped."

"Caroline!" Sally cried. "I know this is bad timing but you and Greg so obviously love each other! You're not trapping him into anything he wouldn't have chosen for himself."

"I'd never know, would I?"

Sally's mouth dropped open. "What are you talking about? The man's crazy about you, and you know it! I can see where this must be hard for you, but don't get so caught up in the memories of what came before that you can't see how different it is from what's happening *now*."

"I'm not caught up," Caroline insisted. "I'm simply not going to let it happen again the same way it did before."

"Seems to me it already has," Sally countered. "At least this time you've been enjoying yourself in the process."

"Not if you mean I've spent the last two and a half months making passionate love, I haven't," Caroline grimaced in utter self-disgust. Then, sighing at Sally's baffled look, she went on to explain, "Greg and I aren't sleeping together. We only made love one night at the end of April. *One night*! Can you believe it! I feel like a freak! The only two times in my life I've given in to, as they say, the heat of the moment, I wind up pregnant. And this time the odds were almost one in a million! Fate's really got it in for me!"

Sally shook her head slowly, awed by the news. "I don't blame you for feeling a little sorry for yourself. And maybe you only need to settle down and get used to the idea before you see that this really doesn't have to be that bad." At Caroline's look of indignation Sally went on quickly. "I mean, come on. Lots of women are having babies in their mid and late thirties these days. You're healthy. Greg's financially comfortable. You've got a good job that you could keep if you wanted to or give up if you decided you'd rather not work. It's not *ideal*, maybe. But it isn't the end of the world."

Caroline was silent for a moment, then said rather curtly, "I suppose it's all a matter of your point of view."

Eight

Caroline's point of view hadn't changed by the time she'd driven home to get ready for an evening out with Greg and the kids. Kim and Rob had invited their parents to dinner weeks ago to celebrate their success with Jeb Stuart; summer jobs and Greg's schedule had postponed the occasion until tonight. And Caroline would have liked to put it off again. She couldn't imagine how she was going to get through the evening until she could talk to Greg privately, but she had little choice.

At seven-thirty she found herself seated at a table in a Chinese restaurant, eating food that she didn't want and drinking water in great quantities.

"Daddy, we never could have done it without you and Ms. Forrester." Kim was bright-eyed and effervescent in a floral print dress with a frothy lace collar. "Rob and I think the two of you deserve most of the credit for our success with Jeb Stuart."

"Yeah," Rob put in. "We know we were a little nuts about this project. You two were really great about taking it seriously. Like, you understood that it was important we go through this thing ourselves, but you knew when it would be okay to help, too."

Having finished his dinner, Greg relaxed in his seat and winked at Caroline across the table. "I don't mind taking my fair share of the credit—which is certainly not most of it. What do you say, Caroline? Don't you think we made first class egg grandparents?"

"Absolutely," Caroline agreed with a thin smile plastered on her lips. She couldn't take this night away from Kim and Rob, no matter how hard it was for her. They'd succeeded admirably where many other students had not, and they deserved a celebration.

"You know, Mom," Rob began, toying with a chopstick as he stared at his empty plate. "I haven't said this much, but I realized, taking care of Jeb, how lucky I've been. I hadn't ever thought about how hard it's been for you, being my mother."

Caroline started to say something, then stopped, realizing she had to let Rob voice his feelings.

"You've had to work twice as hard," Rob continued, still not able to meet his mother's gaze. "Dad's never been there, even when he *was* there—even before your divorce, I mean. I've gotten used to that, pretty much. But I know now that the reason it hasn't really messed me up not to have him around is that you've never let me think I was alone. You've always been there, even when I know you were dead tired from working and going to school and even when it meant you didn't get to do things you might have wanted to do."

He looked over at Kim briefly. "Taking care of Jeb Stuart with Kim showed me a lot about what your life must have been like. It feels like there's no way I could have passed the project alone. I would have lost the egg or broken it or just plain ignored it dozens of times if Kim hadn't been helping me.'' He looked, finally, at his mother. ''I don't know how you did it for so long by yourself. But I'm awful glad you did.''

Caroline knew there were tears forming in her eyes, but she also knew that if she gave in to the almost overwhelming urge to cry, she'd become hysterical.

''Rob,'' she tried to speak, and her voice broke a little. ''I don't know what to say. I...''

''You don't have to say anything, Caroline,'' Greg spoke quietly. ''I think Rob said it all very eloquently.''

Caroline's gaze met his, and he smiled, his own heart nearly bursting with pride for the woman whom he loved so much. He planned to ask her to marry him tonight. His thoughts went to the velvet-lined box in his jacket pocket. On a layover in New York, a friend had introduced him to a jeweler, and he'd bought a ring with a small sapphire mounted in a bed of diamonds. The deep blue stone had instantly reminded him of Caroline's eyes.

When Kim started to speak, Greg's thoughts were on Caroline, and he was, at first, surprised.

''Daddy,'' Kim reached for his hand.

''Yes, princess?''

''I want you to know that Jeb Stuart made me see a lot of things, too,'' she began a little shyly but with great seriousness radiating from her brilliant green eyes. ''I found myself getting scared, thinking about what I'd do if Rob disappeared and I had to take care of, well, our baby, really, alone. I'd lay in bed at night and actually get terrified thinking about it. And it finally occurred to me what it must have been like for you all those years when you knew Mama was going to die and, eventually, you'd have to raise me alone. And it wasn't as if you and she had hated each other and had made a *choice* to have me live with one or the other of you. You loved her and her dying wasn't something you could do anything about. That's exactly what I found the most frightening.''

"It's the unknown that's the worst part, Kim," Greg said, squeezing her hand. "God forbid you'll ever face the same thing, but if you do, I'm confident you'll find the courage and strength to do whatever has to be done."

"But I've made it harder for you to do what *you* had to do," Kim insisted, shaking her head a little. "What I'm trying to say is, I understand now why it's been so difficult for you to let me make my own decisions and to take the consequences of my own mistakes. You've tried to protect me from getting hurt, and all I've done is yell at you and cry and act like a baby. I thought you were deliberately trying to make my life miserable, when all you were doing was telling me you loved me and that you were scared for me. I just spent nine weeks getting absolutely crazed out about a silly egg—something that isn't even alive! And I had Rob to help me! I can't even imagine what it would have been like if that egg had been a real baby!''

Kim shook her head again, obviously overwhelmed. Then she smiled quietly and said, "I love you, Daddy. And I think Ms. Forrester and the person who invented the egg experiment are really excellent, too. If it hadn't been for them, I might not have known until it was too late what it is to get into something and then find out it's not going to be at all like you'd planned. I want you to know that I understand that now. And I want you to know that you don't have to be scared about me anymore."

Greg wondered how he could tell her that a parent never stopped being scared for a child's well-being? He couldn't, he knew. The hard facts were that she'd have to find that out on her own, the same way she'd found out what it was to... to raise an egg.

He looked across the table at Caroline and smiled. "Now that our children have had their say, don't you think it's appropriate for us to tell them what we think of them?"

Caroline sat up a little straighter in her chair and willed her lips to turn upward. "Oh, I agree," she said, wondering what on earth she could say that wouldn't make her feel like an even bigger fool. Rob's and Kim's loving speeches, which they had gone to some pains to present in a fitting manner, hit her where it hurt the most. Everything they'd said seemed to mock her. Words like responsibility and love and fear battered at her weak facade of calm. She felt like a fraud. She felt like the last seventeen years had been an enormous joke. And the joke was on her.

Fortunately, before she had to say anything, Greg spoke.

"I'm sure Caroline shares my feelings in saying that we're very proud of both of you," he began, glancing from one youthful, blushing face to the other. "It might sound a little trite now, but it's true that there's no greater reward for a parent than to have a child say everything you did has been noticed and appreciated. It makes all the sacrifices worthwhile. It makes all the fights and the hard decisions worth the sweat and tears that went into them. And I know that each of you will make a wonderful parent someday, if you choose to be one. You both showed remarkable maturity in how you handled your, uh, pseudoparenthood."

His eyes twinkled a little with amusement as he added, "I must say, it was kind of fun being an egg grandparent and I'm sure I'll enjoy the real thing when it happens. Which I trust will not be any time soon. How about you, Caroline? Don't you look forward to being a grandmother?"

Caroline knew Greg wasn't being deliberately cruel, but she felt like throttling him. "Sure," she replied with a sardonic edge to her voice that she couldn't hide. "Being a grandmother will be swell. I can hardly wait."

Greg frowned a little, confused. Then he chuckled, thinking he must have been wrong in thinking he heard a hidden meaning in her words. "Yeah, a grandparent gets all the rewards of parenting with none of the hassles. No bottles. No diapers. No colic. No worrying about discipline. Just the luxury of being able to indulge a child to the max, every chance you get."

Caroline pushed away from the table and rose. "Excuse me a moment. I'm, uh . . . I'll be right back."

It took her ten minutes in the ladies' lounge to decide she wasn't going to lose her dinner. Whether or not she was going to scream remained to be seen. When she returned to the table, Rob and Kim had already paid the check. The four of them got into the car and rode to the Forrester townhouse. Caroline sat huddled in her seat, feeling beaten and terrified and more angry than she'd ever been in her life.

But the evening wasn't over. They gathered in the living room, and Rob and Kim produced a bottle of champagne that Sally had bought for them. Greg made suitably impressed remarks and didn't offer to help while Rob struggled with the cork. Everyone but Caroline breathed a sigh of relief when the cork popped perfectly and the champagne stayed where it belonged, in the bottle. Rob poured and Kim handed out fluted glasses.

Caroline stared at the fizzing liquid as she listened to her son clear his throat before speaking.

"I'd like to make a toast," Rob began. "To the two most awesome parents in the world. From Kim and me both, this is for understanding and for, well, for being there."

"Here, here!" Kim chimed in.

The chilled glass was actually warm in Caroline's numbed hand. For the second time that day she had the experience of being in an entirely different world. Everything around her simply drifted away as she existed, frozen, in a moment that consisted only of a great swell of painful emotion. Ironically it was the champagne that served as the final straw. She stared at the golden liquid, realizing it was alcohol and therefore off limits for a person in her condition.

I can't drink this, she thought, hazily at first, then with complete clarity as the truth she'd been denying all day sank in. *I can't even drink this!*

With a strangled cry of rage Caroline whirled, and the glass of champagne fell to the carpet as she ran from the room.

"Caroline!" Greg started to rush after her then stopped, realizing Rob and Kim were following. He shot them both a look. "Maybe it would be better if you two waited down here." His tone indicated clearly that his words constituted an order, not a request.

Caroline's door had just been slammed shut when he reached it. He shoved it open and followed her inside, closing the door behind him.

"Greg, please..." Caroline began.

He reached for her. "What is it, honey? What's wrong?"

"Go away!" she sobbed, trying to shove his hands away.

"Not until you tell me what's happened. Are you sick?"

"Yes!" she gasped out, her face in her hands and her back to him. "I'm sick and I'm exhausted and I ache in all the wrong places, and it's not going to get any better! It's only going to get *worse*, until I can't sleep at night and I spend half my life in the bathroom! And, oh, dear God, why did this have to happen *now*?"

"What are you saying?" Greg asked hoarsely, the cold chill of fear creeping up his spine.

"I'm saying I'm *pregnant*!" she cried, throwing his hands off her shoulders with near violent force and whirling to face him. Her face was wet with tears, and her words came in sobbing gulps. "Pregnant! You know. That mysterious state we've been trying to keep Rob and Kim from knowing about too soon. That thing I've spent over two months teaching my students all about. It results in a baby. Not an egg. A real live baby with colic, that cries at night and needs its diapers changed umpteen times a day. The kind of baby you can't send home when you're tired of playing with it and that you can't indulge 'to the max' without paying the consequences for the rest of your life! And I'm—" She hiccoughed and covered her face again. "I'm so tired right now, I want to lay down and die!"

Greg knew his jaw was hanging open, but he was too stunned to do anything about it. Too stunned to move. Speech required the ability to formulate a coherent thought. He stared at Caroline, completely unable to comprehend what was happening.

"But, Caroline," his voice cracked on a whisper. "That's not... You *can't* be!"

"Don't tell me what I can't be, Greg Lawton," she fumed. "I *am*! That stupid operation you had isn't foolproof. And being the ever-fortunate woman that I am, I get to be the fool!"

"Honey, I can hardly believe this. I—"

"I tell you I'm pregnant, and don't you tell me again—"

"No, no," he shook his head. "I believe you. It's just so..." He laughed a little, shaking his head as though it would clear his thoughts. "I mean, I've always known there was that remote possibility, but those aren't the sort of odds one takes seriously. Especially after all these years!"

Greg looked up at her, and suddenly the whole world began to take on a rosy sort of glow. His expression became positively beatific, and he couldn't have stopped the grin from spreading across his face if his life had depended on it.

"Caroline!" He reached out and hauled her stiff form against him, his fingers shaking as they touched her wet cheek. "My darling Carrie, I understand what a shock this must be to you, and I'm sorry you feel so bad. But in my wildest dreams, I never imagined this could happen. It's like a miracle. I can't tell you how happy I am."

"Well, I'm not happy!" Caroline countered, her eyes furious as they met his. "And this sure isn't my idea of a miracle, either!"

"Oh, Caroline, I know it must seem like the cruelest sort of irony to you. You give in to passion twice in your life and both times you get pregnant. But, honey, this isn't like when you were seventeen. I love you! You *must* know that! And all those things I said at dinner about diapers and colic, I was only teasing Rob and Kim. You're not going to be raising this baby alone, like you did Rob. We'll raise it together, and it'll be fun. You'll see."

"It won't be fun!" Caroline's hand came down on his chest, and she pushed away from him. "And I will be alone!"

"No, you won't," he argued patiently as she began to pace the floor in front of her bed. His hand delved inside his jacket pocket and closed over the jewelers box nestled there. "Tonight after we'd finished our party with Kim and Rob, I'd planned to take you to the Potomac overlook above Chain Bridge and ask you to marry me. I'll admit this isn't exactly the romantic little speech I had planned, but Caroline I *do* love you. I want to marry you."

"No," she said flatly. "I won't do it. I won't marry you like this."

Her refusal came as a complete shock. The second one in a very short span of time, this one not so pleasant. Slowly Greg was beginning to get the picture that things were not going to go as he had planned.

"What do you mean, no?" he asked roughly, his fist tightening around the hidden ring box. "Are you saying you don't love me?"

The vulnerable catch in his voice went through her like a knife. Caroline spun toward him, and her eyes, glistening with tears, met his. "No, Greg, I'm not saying I don't love you," she said, her chin trembling. "I love you so much it . . . it almost hurts!"

"Caroline—"

"But I won't marry you!" Again she whirled away, her hands pressing into the sides of her head as though to keep it from bursting apart. "I'm not *ever* going to be forced to marry somebody again. And love . . . love doesn't even have anything to do with it."

"It has *everything* to do with it," Greg countered. By now his nerves were stretched raw, and his heart was pounding. "I love you, and I want to marry you. And I want to raise our baby together. It's that simple."

"It's *not* simple!" Caroline shouted, on the verge of hysteria. "Nothing I do is *ever* simple."

"Caroline, stop it," Greg ordered. "You're going to make yourself sick. We're going to get married because we love each other, and we're going to raise this baby together. And that's that!"

"Ha!" she laughed, bitterly. "*Who's* going to raise this baby together? Me and your housekeeper? Me and Rob? Not me and you, that's for sure. Not when you're gone as many nights as you're home. I'm not going to spend my life sitting around, worrying about where you are when I need you and . . . and who you're with when you're not at home."

The anger inside of him went from warm to boiling. He caught her by the shoulders. "You listen to me, Caroline Forrester. I spent six years being faithful to a woman who was *dying*. Not *once* did I give her cause to wonder whose bed I was sleeping in. And it wasn't because I lacked for choices. I learned about fidelity the hard way. And I won't stand here and have you measure me against some young jerk who'd already proven *before* you married him that he didn't know how to control himself!''

Caroline looked at Greg's furious expression, realized the complete unfairness of what she'd said and dissolved into another sobbing fit. "Oh, Greg, I'm sorry! I don't even know what I'm saying. I know you'd never behave like Chuck in a thousand years. And I know you'd be a good father, and you'd try to be home as much as you could. It's true I hate your schedule, but right now everything seems hundreds of times worse than it really is. I'm so confused and *tired*!'' She hiccoughed several times, her hands fluttering in a gesture of supreme frustration. "I only know that nobody's going to tell me what to do. I already feel like I've lost control of my body. I can't lose control of my life, too.''

In a voice that was flat and cold, Greg bit out, "So, what are you going to do? Raise the baby yourself? You must have some plan in mind.''

"I don't have anything in mind!'' she cried, wondering how long she could stand up under this pressure before she collapsed, literally, to the floor. Pushing away from him, she went to stand by the window. The palms she ran over the front of her linen skirt were wet and she whispered, "I'm scared, Greg. Scared and angry. That's no way to start a marriage. I've spent the last five weeks dreaming about weddings and honeymoons and all the things that *normal* people expect to have when they fall in love. But I'm *not* normal!'' She choked on a short, bitter laugh. "Talk about your wildest dreams! Mine were wild, all right. Wild and foolish. Even these last weeks when I thought everything was wonderful, the whole time I've been pregnant. It's like I've been carrying a bomb around inside of me, ready to self-destruct when I was the least prepared. Well, the bomb has gone off. And I'm the one who's going to have to pick up the pieces.''

She turned to face Greg and her tone became hard and determined. ''And I'm not going to have anybody else—not anybody—tell me how to pick those pieces up. I won't be pressured into marriage or anything else. Right now, I wish you'd just go away and leave me alone. I can't take any more of this.''

Incredulously, Greg shook his head. ''Go away? We've shared everything there is to share with each other. We've practically been living together for weeks. And *now*, when you need me the most, you want me to go away?''

Caroline drew herself up. Amidst all the confusion in her head, something inside her reacted violently at the mention of the word ''need.'' ''I don't need you,'' she said with her chin stuck out and her blue eyes flashing. ''I don't need you or anybody else.''

''Hmph,'' Greg snorted. ''Sure looks to me like you do. You're not making any sense. You haven't been since this conversation began. This isn't exactly the time for you to be by yourself, when you aren't even thinking straight!''

''Don't you dare tell me how I'm thinking,'' she shot back.

''I will tell you,'' he countered. ''That's *my* baby you've got inside you, and I plan to have some say over what happens to it!''

''That's too damned bad. It may be your baby, but it's *my* body. I'm the one who's going to have to change my life. And you're not going to tell me how to do it. Now, will you please go away and *leave me alone*!'' Unable to stand facing him any longer, Caroline whirled back to stare out the window, her vision blinded by tears.

Greg watched her, and as he did, several things were obvious. This should have been a time of joy and happiness; it made him angry that it couldn't be, but he accepted that fact and moved on. Next, arguing was getting them nowhere; he knew that Caroline wasn't thinking rationally. And as his anger cooled, he had to fight back the urge to simply fold her into his arms and try to make it all better.

What was finally becoming clear, however, was that anything he could say or do would only make her feel more pressured than she already did. And that would drive her farther and farther away from him and from accepting the obvious solution to their problem. That it was *their* problem wasn't even an issue. At least, not for him.

However, he also realized that Caroline was right about one thing. He couldn't make this decision for her. He couldn't force her into a marriage she didn't want any more than he'd been able to force her to make love with him. When you loved somebody, you didn't *force* them into anything. As hard as it might be, he was going to have to wait and hope that she did the right thing. The thought that she might actually decide to throw away everything they had was terrifying; it filled him with helpless rage and sadness to think that she might. But a saner part of him realized that he would have to trust her. He couldn't make the choice for her, but he could be there to help her live with the consequences of whatever choice she made. His love for her wasn't going to evaporate, no matter what she decided to do.

The jeweler's box, forgotten for an agonizing minute, was still clutched in his hand. It was like living through an entire lifetime in a moment when he became aware of its presence again. And it took a tremendous act of will to make his fingers unclench and let it go.

With a tired sigh he withdrew his hand from his pocket and walked quietly across the room to Caroline. Placing a hand on her arm, he turned her to face him. His voice was gentle as he spoke. "Caroline, you're absolutely right. This has to be your decision."

Caroline lifted her gaze to Greg's. His words were both a relief and a shock. She didn't want to fight with him anymore, but to have him agree that she would have to make up her own mind made her more frightened than she had been before.

"I'll leave you alone," Greg went on. "And I won't call you or come to see you or bother you in any way. But I want you to remember that I love you very, very much. If you want *or* need me, you only have to say so." And he lowered his mouth to hers, kissing her once briefly. Then he left.

And Caroline stood silently, staring after him.

At the top of the stairs Greg stopped short, his gaze flickering between Rob's and Kim's. The two young people stood in the hallway below, staring up at him wide-eyed. Slowly, one step at a time, he walked down to meet them, wondering what in the world he could possibly say if either of them asked what was wrong with Caroline. When he'd reached the bottom of the stairs, he turned to Rob and started to speak, hoping something sensible would come out of his mouth.

"We heard."

Kim's announcement was uttered in a desperately worried voice. Greg's breath caught for an instant as he glanced at his daughter, then looked more closely at Rob. He wasn't angry at them for eavesdropping. The house wasn't very large, the doors weren't very thick, and he and Caroline hadn't exactly been thinking about who might be listening. But it sure was a rotten way to find out that your mother was pregnant.

"Rob," he began, placing a hand on the boy's shoulder. "Your Mom's upset right now, but she'll be okay."

Rob looked as though he wasn't quite certain. "I don't understand, Mr. Lawton. Why doesn't she—"

"Don't try to make sense of it," Greg cut in. "In fact it would probably be better if you didn't mention anything to Caroline. She wouldn't want to think you'd heard . . . well, that you'd heard her being so upset. Let her tell you the news herself in her own way, when she's ready."

Greg waited until he saw Rob nod reluctantly in agreement. Then he said, "I told Caroline that I wouldn't call her for a while. She wants time to think things through for herself. But it would make me feel a lot better if I heard from you."

Rob lifted his eyes to Greg's and looked at him searchingly. Greg gave him a smile that was meant to be reassuring and maybe even a little conspiratorial. Caroline wasn't up to dealing with all the pressures of new motherhood much less the pressures of old motherhood, yet Rob was going to need somebody to talk to. It seemed reasonable that the two men in this situation could help each other out. "Will you call me and stop by the house whenever you get the chance?" he asked. "If I'm out of town, Kim will always know where to reach me."

"Sure," Rob replied, obviously glad for the opening Greg had given him.

Greg squeezed his shoulder, then turned to Kim. "I think we'd better go home, princess."

Kim nodded. "You go on, Daddy. I'll be there in a minute."

Greg walked to his car, thinking about what an illusion both hopefulness and despair were. The evening, which had begun with so much of the former, was ending with more of the latter than he'd felt in years. Yet neither emotion changed the reality; if anything, they only clouded his rational thinking. Instead of feeling despairing, what he ought to be doing was making plans. In fact if he were smart, he wouldn't give himself time to sit around and worry about what might happen if Caroline decided not to marry him. It would only make him feel worse, and he'd already done everything he knew how to do.

Nine

The cost of independence was high. Caroline had learned that lesson long ago, but she was stoically determined to pay the price. She didn't pretend it was rational. And it made her crazy to be so out of control. She couldn't imagine how her behavior must appear to an outsider, for it was totally incomprehensible even to herself. She loved Greg. Greg loved her. Why couldn't she accept his proposal of marriage and be done with it?

Because try as she might, in her heart, she couldn't really accept the fact that her fate had been taken out of her own hands. Intellectually she knew she was pregnant, that there was life growing within her, but in a way that had nothing to do with rational thought, she rebelled at the knowledge. She'd dreamed of a wedding in a church with roses and long gowns and showers of rice. And in her dreams, there had been an atmosphere of happiness and laughter and much, much love. She didn't care that it might be childish to want a wedding that had all the trappings a *real* wedding should have. She wasn't going to start another marriage "in a hurry." She wasn't going to start another marriage waiting for a baby to be born. She was angry. She felt as if something she'd treasured had been stolen from her. And although she didn't precisely place the burden of her disappointment and resentment on the innocent spark of life she carried, neither did she accept it as a part of herself, something to be loved and nurtured and welcomed.

Her ambivalence tore her apart. She longed to share the burden with Greg, but she couldn't share his joy. And she was afraid to give in to the almost desperate need she felt for him, for fear of losing the last shred of control she had over her life. The more pressure Caroline perceived from the outside to make the obviously sane decision to marry Greg, the more determined she became not to do so. And within a very short period of time, the pressure became fierce.

She didn't know how Rob had learned the news—whether Greg had told him or whether he and Kim had overheard her tirade—but she was certain that he knew. Even if she hadn't seen the knowledge in his curious, concerned glances, she would have been suspicious as to why the garbage was mysteriously disappearing or the laundry being folded and put away without her lifting a finger. Yet, by the end of the week following the celebration fiasco, he still hadn't said anything directly to her. But what really confused Caroline was the fact that Rob talked to Greg almost daily. It shocked her one day when she overheard her adolescent son discussing her health and well-being over the phone in almost clinical terms. She realized immediately that he was talking to Greg and as she listened, she also realized that Rob had been paying more attention to her than he'd let on.

The entire incident shook her badly. Not only did it make her aware of the level of her son's concern, but it reminded her of how horribly she must be hurting Greg. It touched her deeply that, although she'd refused his help and rejected his offer of marriage, Greg continued to show his concern while keeping his promise not to call her directly. The fact that he loved her was evident.

And he wasn't the only one. Caroline was embarrassingly aware that the people who cared about her had formed an alliance on her behalf. It made her extremely uncomfortable, as though she were being backed into a corner. It also made her cry.

What was she *doing*, isolating herself this way? Why couldn't she simply get over her disappointment and resentment and fear, accept this baby and marry its father, whom she loved as deeply as a woman could love a man? On a daily basis she asked herself that question. And each time the answer came back angrily, petulantly: *I won't. I won't. And you can't make me!*

It was Sally who insisted upon pointing out how childish she was being. As if she needed to be reminded.

"Caroline Forrester, you're a fool." Sally plunked down onto one of Caroline's patio chairs and picked up a glass of lemonade from the tray beside her.

It had been two weeks since Caroline had discovered her condition, and Sally had made a point of either seeing her or calling her on the phone every day—in the hopes, Caroline realized, of bringing her to reason.

"I know you're hung up on independence and making it on your own and all that," Sally said bluntly. "But this is ridiculous! You're almost three months pregnant, for pity's sake! Are you going to wait until you go into labor to decide what you're going to do about this baby?"

"Oh, Sally, I don't know what I'm going to do," Caroline replied in utter frustration. Vacation was turning out to be awful. At least teaching summer school had given her something to think about besides the rest of her life. Rob was working full-time mowing lawns, so he wasn't available to distract her, and Sally's visits were not what she considered a distraction.

"While you're making up your mind," Sally went on mercilessly, "you'd better consider how you're going to support this baby. There's no way the school board or the parents will tolerate you teaching at Martha Custis, pregnant and unmarried. It may be against the law to discriminate, but given the position you're in, I'll bet anything they find a way to call it unprofessional behavior and fire you. You could spend years fighting it in court, I suppose, but what would you do in the meantime?" She shook her head ominously. "A health education teacher and developer of the effective parenting curriculum turning up pregnant without benefit of a marriage license? Uh-uh. They'd push you out so fast it would make your head swim—if it isn't swimming already."

"I know," Caroline frowned. "I know I'll have to look for another job."

But had she known it? Had she really considered this ramification of her pregnancy? Or had she ignored that fact along with all the others—like the baby itself or like Greg waiting for her to make up her mind.

"You realize of course that in your misguided attempt to retain some control over your fate, you're dooming yourself to repeating history."

This statement brought Caroline's head around. "What do you mean?"

"Caroline," Sally sighed. "I'm not a psychologist but it's pretty clear to me you're letting fear cloud your good judgment. When you were seventeen, you made a mistake and let a boy who turned out to be a creep get you pregnant. Now you're feeling guilty for being attracted to a *real* man and for letting *him* make you pregnant. You're absolutely terrified that marrying Greg might turn out to be as bad a mistake as it was to marry Chuck Forrester." Sally set her glass of lemonade on the table and leaned forward in her chair. "You could be married to a man who loves you," she went on. "A man who's already proven himself to be a loving father, and who makes enough money so that if you want the luxury of not working outside the home, you can have it. But you're so scared and so guilty about something that happened almost eighteen years ago, you're going to wind up facing motherhood alone. *Again!* I'm sorry, Caroline, but I think what you need is to have your head examined."

Caroline considered it. And then discarded the notion. There wasn't anything anyone could tell her that she wasn't already aware of in vivid detail. She knew she was behaving, at best, irrationally and, at worst, like she'd completely lost her mind.

For another week she went through her daily routine, which consisted of almost frantic housecleaning followed by work on school plans for the following year. All the while her thoughts were in turmoil. At night she lay in bed, missed Greg—and worried.

Reality had a way of tormenting her unmercifully. Sally had talked about her job. She lived in a house with two bedrooms and no conceivable space for a crib—not that there even *was* a crib. And misery of miseries, the day she began her second trimester, the waistband of her favorite pair of shorts no longer snapped.

On the Wednesday afternoon following her third doctor's visit, Caroline came home to find the mail lying on the table in the hall. Thumbing through the day's advertisements and bills, she was surprised to come across a catalog for a local community college. The catalog confused her. Rob had already decided to apply to both Princeton and Yale for early admissions. His grades and test scores were high enough so that he had a good chance of getting in to one or both institutions, though Princeton was his first choice.

As she stood looking at the catalog, Rob came in the front door dressed only in cutoffs and work boots. His hair was wet and curling with sweat, and he looked exhausted.

"Hi, Mom."

"Hi," she replied and added quickly, "I didn't know you were thinking about going to Southern Community College. Did you give up on Princeton?"

He hesitated on his way up the stairs. "Well, you know—" he hedged, speaking over his shoulder "—I thought I'd check out the local scene."

Caroline followed him to his room, stopping in the doorway. "What do you mean, you thought you'd check out the local scene? I thought you'd done that already. I thought you said Princeton had one of the best history departments and that you'd like to try living away from home."

"Yeah, well, a guy can change his mind, can't he?" Rob's comment was casual, but he wouldn't meet her gaze as he flopped down on his bed and picked up an issue of *Rolling Stone*.

"Rob, what's all this about?" she asked insistently.

With a sigh he dropped the magazine onto his chest. "Mom, Ivy League schools cost tens of thousands of dollars. I thought it would be a good idea to look around for something less expensive. I can't afford the big money on my own, and you aren't going to be able to shell it out. So, forget it, huh?"

Aghast, Caroline leaned against the door frame. "You mean you're changing your college plans because I'm going to have a baby?" It was the first time either of them had actually said the word.

"That's what life's about, isn't it?" her son remarked meeting her gaze. "You've made a lot of sacrifices for me. And this is really no big deal. I can spend a few years at Southern, work and save some money, stack up some good grades and try to get a scholarship to a four-year college. If I don't ever get a scholarship, I'll live. Southern may not sound as exciting because I've lived around here all my life, but there's nothing wrong with it. Besides, you're going to need help."

"But, Rob, it's not your job to make sacrifices for me," Caroline argued. "You have a perfect right to expect the very best you can get in a college or in anything else! I won't have you altering your plans for me like this!"

"I guess you don't have much choice about it," he muttered, picking up his magazine once more. "You can make up your mind about your life, but this is one decision *I* can make. And I'm going to make it. How do you think I'd feel being two hundred miles away, knowing you were working to pay for me to go to some overrated school when you couldn't really afford it? Besides this baby is going to be my brother or sister. That means something, doesn't it?" He met her gaze over the top of his magazine. "I want to do this, Mom. Don't feel bad about it. Please."

How could she not feel bad about it? How could she even dream of allowing Rob to make life-altering decisions for her sake? She needed time to think, time to adjust to the major changes her life—and her body—were undergoing; but all around her was evidence that there wasn't any time! She had to face the truth that her dreams of a storybook romance and wedding had been snatched away from her once and for all and that, if she agreed to marry Greg, it would always and forever be true that she'd "had to."

The day following her confrontation with Rob, Caroline was still feeling guilty. It was a sultry August afternoon. Rob was at work; Sally had gone to the ocean for a week with her husband. And in her desperate effort to get away from the chaos inside her by cleaning, Caroline had worked her way to the basement. By three o'clock her cutoffs and T-shirt told a tale of four years of accumulated dust. When the doorbell rang, she looked down at her grubby clothes and decided there wasn't much she could do about it. She dropped the box of rags she was carrying onto the kitchen table, pulled off the scarf she'd tied over her hair and went to answer the door.

The sight of Kim Lawton standing on her front step sent an immediate surge of excitement racing through her. Caroline's first reaction was to look past the girl's shoulders for Greg. When she saw that he wasn't there, her shoulders slumped a little but she offered Kim a friendly smile.

"Can I come in, Ms. Forrester?" Kim asked hesitantly. "My father would kill me if he knew I was here, but I couldn't stand it anymore. I had to come."

Caroline saw immediately that Kim was distraught. She also noticed the girl's dress and patent leather shoes and realized this was a formal visit. "Sure, you can come in," Caroline said, ushering Kim into the living room. "It's nice to see you. Can I get you a soda or some iced tea?"

Kim shook her head and sat down on the edge of the couch. Her lower lip was caught between her teeth, and her fingers were fiddling with her key chain. Caroline sat down beside her.

"Ms. Forrester," Kim spoke nervously. "This probably isn't any of my business, but . . . do you love my father?"

Caroline had to gulp, but she answered immediately, "I love him very much."

Kim's frown was puzzled. "I'm trying to understand, you see, why...why you won't marry him. I know he asked you."

Caroline shifted uncomfortably. A few weeks ago, she'd been thinking of Kim as her future step-daughter, and it struck her even more powerfully than it had with Rob how thoroughly she'd been ignoring other people's feelings.

"Kim," she began, searching for some way to explain the unexplainable. "I don't know if Rob has told you much about his...his early life—"

"I know you were eighteen when you had him," Kim answered, meeting Caroline's gaze. "Rob thinks that's why you're so committed to the effective parenting unit at Martha Custis. He thinks you've sort of, well, dedicated your life to preventing kids from getting in trouble the way you did."

"I don't know that I've dedicated my life to the cause," Caroline said slowly, "but I certainly feel it's important work for me to be doing. Anyway you know that I, as they say, had to get married to Rob's father. And I imagine Rob's told you what sort of marriage that was. We didn't love each other. We were only married out of guilt and necessity. But Kim, even if we *had* loved one another, the circumstances of being pregnant before the wedding—that's a serious handicap to overcome. It's no way to begin *any* marriage. I...I suppose that I feel like marrying your father under those circumstances is really dooming us from the start."

Skepticism was plainly stamped on Kim's delicate features. "Are you sure there isn't something else? Maybe something I've done that makes you think being married to Daddy would be a bad thing?"

"Oh, Kim, no!" Caroline replied instantly. "Of course it isn't you."

Kim shrugged a little. "I thought maybe you might be worried that I'd be jealous of having to share him with you and the new baby. And I even wondered if you were worried about my mother—about whether Daddy still loves her. I know I said some things the night we all went out to dinner that made it sound like he must have loved her an awful lot."

"I know he did," Caroline said gently. "It's never occurred to me to be jealous of your mother, Kim. I know your father and mother had a wonderful marriage, and it's always seemed to me that his loving her has made him a better person."

Caroline heard herself speaking thoughts that she'd never completely formulated in her own mind before. She was being forced to do so now because she couldn't allow Kim to think that it was her fault—or the fault of her mother whom she loved—that her father's marriage proposal had been rejected. "Love isn't a contest, Kim," she went on to say. "You don't go around wondering whether somebody loves you more or less than they love—or have loved—somebody else. And if you're smart, you realize that people grow best by having more than one person whom they love. You don't get jealous of their other relationships and you trust them to honor whatever bargains they've made with you."

"You mean like being faithful and all," Kim concluded.

"Yes, like that."

Kim was quiet for a minute. Then, still searching for some plausible explanation for Caroline's refusal to marry her father, she said, "Well, if you're not jealous of my mother, and you *must* know Daddy loves you, are you worried about his being away so much? It's bothered me, too, sometimes, but Mrs. Reid's always been there, and I love her a lot, too. And the last couple of years, I've had enough other stuff to keep me from thinking about it much. But I realize it would be different—being married to him, I mean—if he were gone half the time. And especially if you had a baby to take care of, too.''

Caroline didn't try to lie about how she felt. ''It's certainly something I've thought about. His schedule is so erratic. It would be hard to know what I could depend on. But really, Kim, that's the least of my concerns.''

''It won't always be so bad,'' Kim insisted, her eyes almost pleading. ''He's working so hard to qualify for 747 status when the next position opens up. Right now he's got the top cockpit position on a smaller jet, and there's only four other pilots with the same seniority at TCA. If he can get higher seniority, he wouldn't be away half as much and he'd be making more money. He could have had those hours logged over a year ago, but he hasn't wanted to be away from me all the time, so he's put it off. I'm sure he's decided to do it now because he wants to be able to be around when the baby is born, in case—'' she lowered her gaze ''—in case you change your mind about marrying him, that is.''

It didn't surprise Caroline that Greg had made such a decision without telling her. It was like Rob deciding to apply to Southern Community College instead of to a private university. These unsolicited sacrifices were killing her. She didn't *want* Greg to wear himself out working for a promotion to make her more comfortable about his schedule. She didn't want him to do *anything* to prove how much he loved her or how willing he was to make sacrifices on her behalf. He'd already done more than enough.

''Well,'' Kim sighed, bringing Caroline's attention back to her. ''I guess I don't understand. Daddy's been so lonely. It's kind of hard to figure out how come, if you really love him, you can let him go on being that way.''

Kim hadn't outright said she was mad, but her feelings and her confusion were obvious in the hardening of her mouth and the way she couldn't quite meet Caroline's gaze. Caroline couldn't think of a response. What was there she could say? If she were Kim, she'd be angry, too. Her level of guilt about what she was putting Greg through reached zenith proportions.

Kim went on, "Daddy worries about you all the time. And so does Rob. Even Mrs. Reid asks Rob how you are every day when he calls or comes by."

"I'm not trying to make them worry, Kim," Caroline said quietly, knowing that in another minute she'd be crying. "The truth is, I'm worried about myself."

Kim continued as though she hadn't heard Caroline speak. "I called Mrs. Stimpson last week and talked to her about how I felt and about why you were... acting like you're acting. I told her I thought maybe you were embarrassed about... well, about getting pregnant and being the sex education teacher and all. She didn't seem to think that was the major problem for you. But she told me you were upset because of your age and because raising a baby isn't what you'd planned to be doing at this time in your life. I talked to Daddy about it, and he agreed. He also said that every woman has a right to expect control of her own body and that she should be able to choose when she has a baby. I understand all that. But I don't think *anybody* has the right to make a choice that hurts so many people!"

Kim's voice cracked on her last words, and she looked around a little frantically, as though ashamed of having Caroline see how truly upset she was. "Ms. Forrester," she continued as the tears started streaming down her cheeks. "I know you're upset about Daddy making you pregnant when it never should have been able to happen. And I guess I'd be upset, too, if I were in your position. It must feel like starting over, when you've already got a son who's sixteen and then find out you're going to have a *new* baby to be even *more* responsible for! I guess I'd feel pretty miserable about the whole thing if it were me. But I don't understand how you can hurt Daddy this way by not letting him love you, not letting him help when he wants to *so much*! You're not even giving him the chance to have this baby to raise when I know he wants it real bad!"

"Kim," Caroline began and tried to put her arm around the girl's shoulders.

Kim avoided the embrace, jumping up off the couch to stand stiffly a few feet away. "And you're hurting Rob, too!" she continued. "He's not going to get to go to Princeton or Yale like he wants to. He says he doesn't care, but I know he'd really like to go *somewhere* better than Southern! If you married Daddy, I'm sure he'd want to help put Rob through college. I'm sure he'd want to do everything he could to make Rob feel like he finally had a man who cared about him, like a father should. I know Rob says he's too old to care anymore, but you know that's not true! And I'm—" she dropped her gaze and hiccoughed a little "—I'm not too old, either, to want a...well, I was starting to look forward to...to having you, you know?"

"Oh, Kim," Caroline's breath caught on a tiny sob. "I was looking forward to it, too. I'd be so proud to be able to call you my daughter. And I know Rob and your dad have made all kinds of sacrifices for me that I never wanted them to have to make. I know it's hurting them to make them but—"

"No, it's *not*!" Kim interrupted shaking her head furiously. "Daddy's working extra hard and Rob's changing his school plans isn't *hurting* them. What hurts is that you won't accept what they're trying to do! Making a sacrifice for somebody you love doesn't *hurt*. You don't think about what you're denying yourself. It's just a...a choice you make."

A sacrifice is just a choice you make.

The words rang over and over in Caroline's mind as she stared at Kim. And suddenly, in one stunning blow, it hit her what a complete fool she was being. She was *choosing* to sacrifice Greg's love, a love she needed and wanted with all her heart—in return for what? What was she gaining? What was *anyone* gaining?

Nothing. Absolutely nothing. And what on earth was the point of a sacrifice if no one benefited from it having been made?

All this time she'd been feeling cheated out of having control over her life, cheated of the opportunity of going into a marriage with Greg with a clear mind and heart. Cheated out of some storybook notion about how love and marriage *ought* to happen. And all the while she'd closed her mind to how badly she was cheating them all. It was as Kim had said. She was keeping Rob from going to the college of his choice. She was snatching away Kim's chance to have a woman to turn to as she might have turned to her mother. She was depriving herself and Greg of each other's love and the chance for happiness they both deserved. And she was cheating everyone of the opportunity to know and love this baby.

The baby. Oh, dear Lord, *the baby!*

In a single moment of blinding awareness, Caroline felt the reality sink down inside her—and settle. And it settled right where it belonged, inside the warmth and protection of her womb. Her hand crept off the arm of the couch and covered her belly as a wave of some indescribable emotion washed through her, saturating her entire being with wonder and protectiveness. And love.

How could she have denied this baby her love for so long? How could she have even considered cheating it of its father's love? This was Greg's baby, his miracle baby, his one in a million chance that had, against such impossible odds, found its life inside her body. It was a gift. And she was in awe of its beauty.

In the space of a single breath the resentment and anger that had filled Caroline for weeks were replaced by a much stronger emotion. The guilt she'd created inside herself by acting so foolishly disappeared, and her sense of purpose returned along with her sanity.

Fairy tales were for children. She didn't need a three-tiered wedding cake. The only thing she needed was Greg's precious, enduring love. And it was hers. All she had to do was claim it.

Ten

Traffic on the access road out of Dulles Airport seemed crazier than usual. Greg drove mechanically, trying to avoid an accident. His uniform shirt was pulled open at the neck, and his tie hung unknotted; his hat and jacket were tossed carelessly across the back seat. There was a stubble of beard on his face. He'd spent a hundred hours in the cockpit over the last four weeks, and every one of them showed. But the last flight had given him the edge he needed to qualify for jumbo jet status.

Not that it would do him any good. He'd been working hard in the hopes that Caroline would come to her senses and call him. When she hadn't, he'd kept working anyway because he didn't know what else to do. And flying helped take his mind off painful subjects—how much he missed Caroline, how worried he was about her and how incredibly hurt and bitter he felt.

How long could he go on like this? he wondered. How long could he hold out before he gave in to the overpowering need to talk to her? He couldn't accept that he was going to have to let her go. He couldn't believe she was actually going to throw their love away as though it had meant nothing. He reasoned he could last until the end of August. Then, promises be damned, he would call her and try to talk to her again.

Did she remember that he loved her? Had she ever really believed it?

Greg pulled into his driveway and frowned when he saw that Kim's car was missing. This was Mrs. Reid's weekend off. That meant the house was empty. He almost backed the car out of the drive to find dinner where he wouldn't have to be alone, but in his current state of mind he figured he'd do more drinking than eating. What he really needed was some food and a bed. A shower and shave wouldn't hurt, either.

His first surprise came when he opened the front door and smelled something cooking. Something very tempting. Probably, he thought, Mrs. Reid or Kim had made dinner for him before leaving.

The next surprise stopped him in his tracks. He paused in front of the archway leading to the dining room. The table was set for two. Candles were burning, and a bottle—no, two bottles—of champagne were cooling in an ice bucket.

His curiosity kept pace with the racing of his heart as he walked slowly toward the kitchen. The sight of Caroline, bent over the open oven door, made his breath catch in his throat and his palms grow instantly damp. Her honey-brown hair was loose around her shoulders and had fallen forward to hide her face. The rose-colored sheath she was wearing was molded softly to the gentle curve of her bottom. Her stockinged feet were bare.

"Caroline?"

She looked up startled, pushing the bangs off her forehead with the back of her hand. "Greg! I didn't hear you come in."

He took two steps toward her. "What—" His voice cracked, and he cleared his throat. "What are you doing?"

She closed the oven door and shrugged a little. "Cooking your dinner."

He took two more steps across what had suddenly become an endless stretch of floor. "Where's Kim?"

"At the beach." Caroline's eyes locked with his. "With Rob. And Mrs. Reid."

"I see." Did he see? Was this setup everything it appeared to be? He hardly dared to hope. "Caroline, what—"

"You've got time before dinner to shower if you'd like." Caroline cast her gaze around the room until she located her shoes under the kitchen table, then, slipping them on, moved hurriedly toward the sink. She'd been nervous all day but the sight of Greg actually standing in front of her made her tremble all over. Ridiculously she wondered if he'd think her little surprise was foolish.

Foolishness was the farthest thing from Greg's mind, ranking right after showers and changing his clothes, but he checked his instinctive movement toward Caroline. Patience had gotten him this far and hopefully it would take him the rest of the way. His prospects were looking up more and more with each passing second.

"I won't be long," he said, still unable to take his eyes off her.

"You've got plenty of time," she said softly, gazing at him for a long moment.

Finally she looked away. "Dinner will be ready in a half hour."

He had to force himself to stop gaping and walk slowly out of the room, but once he reached the front hall, he bounded up the stairs and into his bedroom, ripping his shirt off as he went. Every second it took him to shower and dress, he had to tell himself that Caroline would still be there when he went back down.

The thought of escape did cross Caroline's mind very briefly. The twenty-four hours since Kim's visit had been passed in making plans, and as the hours had gone by, tiny fears had begun to haunt her. Had Greg become so frustrated with her irrational behavior that he'd lost all the good feelings he'd had about her? He looked exhausted. His tan had faded, the lines at the corners of his eyes were more pronounced, and there was a wounded look about those crystal-gray eyes that spoke of pain. She took the blame for that. She remembered the expression that had come over his face after she'd told him about the baby—such a look of joy as she'd never seen before. And it was her heartfelt desire to see his eyes lit with that emotion once again.

"Can I help?" Greg said as he came up behind her, startling her for the second time since he'd arrived home. She almost dropped the salad, but he caught it. "Sorry. Did I scare you?"

"Yes. I mean, no. Not really."

Their eyes locked as they both held onto the teakwood bowl; an endless moment, full of questioning silence, passed.

"Do you want me to put this on the table?" he asked finally.

She nodded. "Would you, please?"

"I will if you let go of it."

Caroline looked down at the lettuce and tomatoes and then back up at him. He smiled down at her.

"You look beautiful, Caroline."

"So do you."

"No, I don't. I look like hell."

"Not to me."

Greg's gaze took note of the pots on the stove and the steaming basket of corn muffins. "This all smells wonderful."

Blinking, Caroline pulled herself together, determined to do this exactly the way she'd planned. The right way.

"It's ready," she said. "Help me put it on the table, and we can eat."

When the meal was served, Greg held Caroline's chair for her and then reached for one of the bottles of champagne. "You must be planning on a long evening," he remarked, gesturing toward the other bottle.

"That's his and her champagne," she explained, a tiny smile tugging at the corners of her mouth. "One of them is nonalcoholic."

Greg looked at the bottle he held. "Is this because you think I've got to fly soon?"

"No, I know you're home for the weekend. But I'm not drinking alcohol."

He looked at her, and slowly, comprehension dawned. "Because of the baby. I guess it makes sense you'd be a stickler for—" He broke off. "*That's* why the champagne upset you so badly that night. You couldn't drink it."

Caroline felt a blush creep into her cheeks. She looked away. "I'd rather not think about that night, Greg. In fact—" she gestured toward the table and its elegant trappings "—this is supposed to make up to you for what happened then."

"Caroline, I—"

"Please, Greg." She lifted pleading eyes to his. "Let me finish. I . . . I spoiled that evening for everybody. I'm not blaming myself exactly—I was terribly upset, and I think I did the best I could do at the time—but I want to try to...to do it again. The way it should have been done. If you'll let me."

If he'd let her? Dear Lord, *if he'd let her!*

"How would you like it to be, Caroline?" he asked, his voice rough and low and shaking.

"I'd like you to pour that champagne and then, sit down and enjoy this dinner with me."

Two corks had never left their bottles with such efficiency. Greg poured their separate drinks and sat down.

"Caroline, I don't know how to tell you this, but I'm not sure I can eat right now." Greg looked at the Crab Imperial, baked rice and vinaigrette salad thinking it might as well have been a hamburger and fries.

"You'll feel hungry once you start eating," she told him, though she felt the same way. Forcing herself to pick up her fork, she began to eat.

With a sigh Greg followed suit.

The meal passed in utter silence, but the looks they exchanged were eloquent.

It's been so long.

I've needed you so badly.

I want to hold you. Kiss you.

Please. Be patient a little longer. You'll see.

As the dinner progressed, it took on an almost ritualistic quality. Their movements became slow and sensual, though not deliberately so. The air had a languorous, peaceful feel to it. It was the sort of atmosphere that seeped into the bones, making one believe there was all the time in the world, that there was nothing more important to do than exactly what was being done. Each second that passed was infused with a richness that filled the senses. The food began to taste better than anything either of them had ever eaten. The smells in the room seemed especially fragrant. The sound of glasses clinking and silverware tinkling softly against china were strangely melodious. When the meal finally came to an end, it had worked a kind of magic on the two lovers who had partaken of the ceremony.

Caroline waited until Greg had finished, then removed the dishes, returning from the kitchen with two scalloped desert plates. Hers had a slice of Black Forest cake topped with whipped cream—of which she didn't expect to take a single bite. Greg's plate was covered with an inverted rice bowl.

Greg eyed the two dissimilar plates closely, then lifted his gaze to meet Caroline's.

Carefully with her eyes never wavering from his, she said, "The night that we celebrated with Kim and Rob, I made several very bad mistakes. First I stole your chance to ask me to marry you in the way you had intended, and I stole your right to hear the answer from me that you should have heard."

"Caroline, you haven't stolen anything from me," Greg tried to tell her. "You were hurting far more than I."

She shook her head. "It's done with, Greg. We can't go back and have it the way it should have been. And you shouldn't have to ask me twice to marry you when once should have been enough. So this time it's my turn." She nodded toward his plate. "Take off the cover."

His hand shook a little—and then a lot—as he lifted the blue porcelain bowl and discovered a small, black jeweler's box. It was very much like the one he had lying in his top dresser drawer.

"Open it," she said.

It crossed his mind that a very rare gift was being bestowed upon him. Countless millions of women had been given occasion to open little boxes like the one he held, but he wondered how many men had been treated to such an experience. A smile crossed his lips as he flipped the box open to find a man's gold dinner ring set with a striking tigereye.

"Caroline, it's beautiful," he said shakily, thinking it could have been a piece of plastic from a gumball machine and he'd have felt the same way.

"They don't make matched sets of engagement rings and wedding bands for men," she continued. "But I bought a band to go with that ring that I thought you'd like. And I was hoping that, seeing as how I love you so much, you would consider wearing it. Will you marry me, Greg? Will you share your life with me?"

"Oh, Caroline," he shook his head slowly, feeling the unfamiliar sting of tears in his eyes. "My darling Carrie, nothing in this world would make me happier than sharing my life with you. Yes, I'll marry you. And I hope you want to do it soon because I can hardly sit here and talk when all I'm thinking about is holding you and loving you."

An incredibly beautiful smile appeared on her face. "I hadn't planned to make either of us wait until we're married to, shall we say, exercise our conjugal rights. But—" her look stopped him from reaching for her then "—there's one more thing I want to say first."

"Can you make it quick?"

She laughed softly and reached for the ring. Taking it out of its box, she reached for his hand and slipped it onto the proper finger. The ring fit, as she knew it would, and she studied it for a moment before lifting her eyes to his.

Her face was vulnerable and had the look of a woman in love as she said, "There was something else I stole from you that night in my room. I can't give you back the . . . the surprise and newness of it, but I still want to say this the way it should have been said then." Her eyes melted softly into his.

"Greg, darling, I'm going to have your baby. And I'm so happy."

He did reach for her then, and for a long while the only sounds in the room were their whispered endearments and breathless words of love. They kissed and touched and kissed again, both of them filled with unspeakable happiness.

"You really are happy about the baby?" Caroline asked, knowing the answer but wanting to hear it again.

"Oh, God, Caroline," Greg sighed against her lips. "You can't begin to imagine how happy I was...how happy I *am*." He pulled back to gaze down at her, his hands cupping her face. "If you had looked for years, searched the entire face of the earth, you couldn't have found a gift that would have brought me more joy. Except one. And I've got you now, too."

"Greg, I love you," she whispered, bringing his lips back to hers.

He kissed her long and deeply, then dragged his mouth across her cheek and buried it against her neck. "Are the kids away for the whole weekend?"

"Hmm-mmm. With strict orders not to be back until Monday morning."

"They know about all this?"

"Kim helped me cook most of the day."

"Oh, honey, it feels so good to hold you!"

"Greg, can we go upstairs now? I don't think I can stand up much longer with you touching me like that, and floors don't appeal to me much these days."

He led her to his bedroom then, and after pulling back the spread of the big bed, he turned to her, removing her hands from the buttons she was undoing and replacing them with his own. He opened her dress slowly, stopping frequently to kiss the soft skin that was revealed.

Caroline stood quietly, the blood racing in her veins and her breathing becoming more and more ragged under his touch. When he'd removed the last of her garments and she stood naked before him, a wave of shyness washed through her.

Greg's heated gaze swept over her, and his hand reached out to touch her breast as he breathed, "Oh, Lord, Caroline. You're so beautiful."

Her breasts were swollen, the nipples darkened by her pregnancy. They both watched as he traced the outline of one crest with his finger. It hardened instantly under the light caress. When his hand smoothed down her ribs and came to rest on the small mound that was his child, his eyes came up to meet hers. And for the first time in her life Caroline knew what it was to experience the infinite love of the man whose baby she carried. The beauty, the almost unbearable intimacy of it made her tremble and left her weak.

"Caroline," Greg whispered, his eyes locked with hers as his hand smoothed across her belly. "Caroline, you're going to have my baby. You really are."

"Yes, I really am," she whispered back, then went on almost desperately. "Oh, Greg, I've missed you so badly. I want to love you! I *need* to love you!" Her fingers shook as she reached for the buttons of his light blue shirt.

Greg didn't help her but threw back his head and reveled in the feel of her hands running over his chest. She quickly pushed the shirt off his shoulders. "Oh, yes, Caroline. Touch me. Please, touch me!"

Her lips joined her hands and soon he was sucking in his breath as the delicate, infinitely sensual caress of her mouth made the blood pool in his loins. When he reached for the buckle of his belt, she waited until he had his slacks unzipped, then put her hands on his hips to push his pants and briefs to the floor. Her mouth followed the trail her fingers made across his ribs and flat belly and down his thickly muscled thighs. Then slowly her hands cupped the fullness of him, and he felt her lips, soft and loving.

"Caroline! My God, I want you! I want to be inside you. I want to feel you all around me!"

He scooped her up against him, and somehow he found the bed. His mouth was feverish and wet and hungry as he covered her, all of her, with kisses. But, when his journey brought him to the gently rounded swell of her belly, he paused. His gaze was alight with wonderment and awe as he lifted it to hers. His touch was almost reverent.

There was a kind of vulnerability and excitement in the trembling of his fingers that made Caroline wonder how on earth she ever could have thought to deprive them of this moment. She knew her cheeks were wet with tears but she felt no embarrassment at his frankly curious exploration of her body. It was a strange, new eroticism, and she gloried in it. It seemed a miracle that they should be sharing this moment when neither of them had expected to have such a gift bestowed upon them again. Not in their wildest dreams...

Finally, Greg's exploration of Caroline's lush softness took him further—to her breasts, her thighs and the moist heat between them. She was soon whimpering with need, and he moved to fuse their flesh into one. Carefully, not letting any of his weight rest on her abdomen, he cradled her hips in his hands and lifted her to him.

Caroline gasped as he entered her, her fingers clutching his shoulders. "Greg! Oh, you feel so good. So good."

"We feel good together," he told her hoarsely, then buried his face against her neck. "Lord, Carrie, I can't wait! I've got to—"

"Darling, please," she begged, arching to meet him. "Love me."

And he did. Until she was crying out his name as the throbbing waves of fulfillment surged through her. He felt them too, and held her tightly, joining her in that special place of deep, abiding intimacy and endless pleasure.

When he collapsed, it was to roll to his side and take her with him. For a long while they lay still while their breathing slowed and the last ripples of pleasure quivered through them. Occasionally a finger would snake its way through a stray curl. Once in a while lips would graze lightly over flesh made slick by passion's heat.

Finally Greg's mouth curved into a lazy smile. "The whole weekend, huh?"

Caroline opened her eyes and met his peaceful gaze. "What?"

"We've got all weekend. Alone."

She smiled back. "Uh-huh. You got plans?"

"Oh, a few. I'm thinking about all the ways we can make love that I won't have to worry about crunching the, uh...egg."

Caroline giggled. "Funny thing about this egg. As long as it's where it is right now, it's practically shatterproof. You'd have to work awfully hard to get it to crunch."

"Let's not tell the kids that."

"They already know."

"They do?"

"They'd better. It was part of the effective parenting curriculum."

"Just so they haven't been trying a few experiments on their own."

"Not a chance," Caroline said smiling. "Rob told me a long time ago that he and Kim stopped thinking of each other romantically after our weekend at the beach together. They're simply very good friends."

Greg's expression was clearly surprised. "What happened to the hot romance?"

"Us," she replied. "They talked it over and decided that it looked like a pretty good possibility they'd end up living in the same house as stepbrother and stepsister. They decided that should such a situation develop, they wouldn't want to know *too* much about each other—as Rob put it."

Greg stared at her for a moment, then burst into laughter. "Smart kids we've got, Caroline."

"I remember thinking so at the time," she agreed, laughing with him, "though I must admit, it shocked the daylights out of me."

"Are you still shocked?"

"That we've got smart kids?"

"That you're lying here with me and pregnant."

"A little," she smiled. "Nothing like this has ever happened to me before. It takes some getting used to, being this happy."

"I'll give you all the time you need," his voice rumbled in her ear as his hips moved against hers in a renewal of passion. "I've recently discovered that patience has some pretty incredible rewards."

And he reaped them all during the night...and the day...and the night that followed.

By Sunday morning they were both ready to share their exuberance with the rest of the world. They went on a trip to a local shopping mall and browsed through the infant departments of every store they could find. Greg insisted on buying Caroline a T-shirt with the words "Under Construction" across the oversize front—though Caroline swore he was crazy if he thought she'd wear it. In the bookstore they loaded themselves down with books about childbirth, and in a small gift shop they purchased a crib mobile with hearts and rainbows and unicorns all exquisitely stitched in needlepoint.

On the way home from the mall Greg rented movies, and they spent the evening watching *The African Queen*. Caroline fell asleep on the couch while Rosy and Charlie battled the raging river in Charlie's old boat. Greg carried her to bed.

Monday morning over breakfast, Greg brought up the topic of Caroline's medical care. Finally able to satisfy his curiosity about all the things he'd been missing, he asked, "Have you made any plans yet for the birth?"

Caroline nodded. "I'm seeing the midwife who taught my classes last semester on prenatal nutrition. I've known Linda since college, and I trust her completely. The doctor she works with will be at the hospital in case of emergency, but unless complications develop, she can deliver the baby and we can use a birthing room for labor and delivery. It's as close to being in your own bedroom as you can get, right down to the TV and the Jacuzzi! The best part is that the baby won't ever have to leave us after it's born."

Greg's eyes widened. "Did I hear you say *us*?"

She grinned. "Things have changed a little, darling, since Rob and Kim were born. You can be with me from beginning to end. That is, if you want to be."

"If I *want* to be!" he exclaimed. "I'll make damned sure I don't have to fly any farther than Cleveland within two weeks in either direction of when you're due. You bet I'm gonna be there."

Caroline frowned a little. "Can you arrange that? I didn't know you had any control over your schedule."

"I've always had some control. But after the first of September I'm hoping to have a lot more. I've finally moved into a position to qualify to sit in the captain's seat in a 747. I should get first pick of the routes when the pilots bid on scheduling each month, which is a whole lot better than getting the leftovers. I probably won't be away overnight half as much as I have been. Come to think of it, I could put in for some of the vacation time I've got coming, then I'll be certain of being here when you need me.''

"That's wonderful," Caroline said and meant it. She'd already decided she could live with his schedule, but it was delightful to hear it wouldn't be as bad as she'd thought.

At that moment they both heard the front door open.

"Looks like the honeymoon's over," Greg commented, returning Caroline's grin of anticipation. "The troops have arrived."

A moment later Kim's head appeared in the doorway.

"They're in here!" she called excitedly over her shoulder and then took a hesitant step into the room.

Rob appeared in a rush, coming to a halt behind Kim. Both of them looked from Caroline to Greg, and the question in their eyes couldn't have been more obvious.

Greg laughed and Caroline said, "It's safe, you two. Come on in."

"Is it... Are you...?" Rob began.

Greg grabbed Caroline's hand and held it up flashing their respective engagement rings before a rapt audience. "Looks like you two are going to have to start sharing a bathroom," he said beaming.

The shrieks of delight that followed the announcement were deafening, and the next few minutes consisted mainly of hugs and kisses and incomprehensible, excited chatter.

Finally Kim ran from the room calling, "I'll be right back. I have to get something."

When she returned, she was carrying a manila folder. Casting a quick, secretive look at Rob, she walked slowly up to Caroline.

"I hope you don't take this wrong," she began shyly and with a hint of concern. "If you don't like the idea, that's okay. But, well, I thought you might. Anyway, I asked a friend of mine to make this for me last Thursday—after our talk."

Caroline stared down at the folder Kim handed her. Unable to imagine what was inside, she glanced at Greg, who smiled and shrugged his ignorance. Curiously and with a little rush of nervous anticipation she opened the folder.

For an instant her breath caught as she scanned the careful lettering on the ivory parchment before her.

Mr. Robert Forrester and Ms. Kimberly Lawton
request the honor of your presence
at the marriage of their parents
Caroline Anne
and
Gregory Charles
on Saturday, September third

And that was as far as Caroline got before she burst into tears.

Epilogue

The house was silent and dark as Caroline and Greg entered and walked quietly up the stairs toward their bedroom. The only light came from the soft glow of the night lamp left burning in the nursery. On their way down the hallway Caroline started to motion to Greg that she was going to check Jennifer before following him to bed, but the sound of quiet voices stopped them both outside the nursery door. Peeping inside, they found Rob and Kim standing side by side, leaning against the crib railing.

"Aren't we going to wake her up?" Rob queried softly of his stepsister.

"You know she'll sleep until she's hungry," Kim answered confidently. "I hope they're having a good time. It's hard to get out for an evening with a nursing baby."

Rob snorted softly. "Are you kidding? They always have

a good time together. It even makes me feel old, the way they play."

"I think they're wonderful."

"I hope I'm that wonderful when I'm that old! I don't think they've stopped kissing since the day they got married."

"Rob, that's crude."

"Well, it's true."

With a wistful sigh, Kim changed the subject. "Isn't she pretty?"

"Yeah," Rob answered softly. "I'm glad I'm going to Georgetown University in the fall. It's been almost a year but I'm still not used to having a family like this. It beats anything Princeton or Yale could have given me."

Kim chuckled softly. "Well, I'm glad you aren't going away, too, because I'd be left with all the babysitting! Mark wouldn't like that one bit."

"Yeah? Well, you can tell Mark Saranson to cool it," Rob growled. "He's getting a little overanxious anyway, if you ask me."

"Oh, Rob," Kim sighed, clearly exasperated. "You're starting to sound like Daddy used to sound. I can take care of myself."

"Well, I worry, that's all," Rob grumbled. "If Saranson starts dishing out anything you can't handle, you let me know. Okay?"

There was a short silence.

Then Kim's voice came softly in the semidarkness. "I love you, Rob."

Another moment of quiet passed before Rob answered. "I love you, too."

And in the hallway those same words were echoed— though with very different intent—by Caroline and Greg, who stood wrapped in each other's arms watching their present joys and their future hopes grow before their loving eyes.

* * * * *

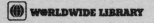

D Silhouette Desire

COMING NEXT MONTH

AVAILABLE NOW:

COMING NEXT MONTH

Silhouette Classics

The best books from the past by
your favorite authors.

The first two stories of a delightful collection...

#1 DREAMS OF EVENING by Kristin James

As a teenager, Erica had given Tonio Cruz all her love, body and soul,
but he betrayed and left her anyway. Ten years later, he was back in her
life, and she quickly discovered that she still wanted him. But the
situation had changed—now she had a son. A son who was very much
like his father, Tonio, the man she didn't know whether to hate—or love.

#2 INTIMATE STRANGERS by Brooke Hastings

Rachel Grant had worked hard to put the past behind her, but Jason
Wilder's novel about her shattered her veneer of confidence. When they
met, he turned her life upside down again. Rachel was shocked to
discover that Jason wasn't the unfeeling man she had imagined. Haunted
by the past, she was afraid to trust him, but he was determined to write a
new story about her—one that had to do with passion and tenderness
and love.